# THE PHILOSOPHER'S
# MURDER CASE

# THE PHILOSOPHER'S
# MURDER CASE

## Jack R. Crawford

COACHWHIP PUBLICATIONS

Greenville, Ohio

*The Philosopher's Murder Case*, by Jack R. Crawford
© 2014 Coachwhip Publications
Jack Randall Crawford, 1878-1968
No claims made on public domain material.
First published 1931.
Cover: Statue, Aachen, Germany © Jens Lind

ISBN 1-61646-251-5
ISBN-13 978-1-61646-251-2

CoachwhipBooks.com

# CONTENTS

# I
## PARK AVENUE AT SEVENTEEN MINUTES TO SEVEN

IT WAS EXACTLY seventeen minutes to seven when Julia burst into my apartment. I noticed the time particularly because Evans had just given me warning that he was going to serve dinner in a few minutes, and I had glanced at my watch, wondering why he made his announcement ahead of time. My instructions were positive that he was not to notify me until fifteen minutes to seven. I was in the middle of a note on the edge of my manuscript to the effect that the uneducated have no conception of the value of time, when Julia swept aside the protesting Evans and stood before me.

Time was, of course, when I should have been surprised to have a young and beautiful girl force her way in—at least, the expression on Evans' face indicated that he had protested her entry—force her way in, I was saying, to my bachelor apartment. But times have indeed changed, I reflected, and there is only Evans and his tribe of old time servants left who see anything odd in such behavior.

It was, nevertheless, awkward, because Julia's only relative, her uncle Howard, was forever abandoning his niece to attend directors' meetings and leaving me the task of amusing Julia. And tonight I had promised to go on to the theatre with the Gordon Trues at eight fifteen, an appointment which had caused me to set my own dinner forward some half an hour. Normally, of course, I did not dine before seven thirty and Evans' warning was usually timed for seven fifteen. I mention this particularly because so many casual persons neglect the importance of time. It is absolutely essential to account for every second, if one is to plan a day properly. Now it was certain Julia had called to take me somewhere, and here was I all tied up for the Gordon True's theatre party. It was always extremely difficult to persuade Julia to alter her plans in order to accommodate any one else, especially an elderly friend like me who existed principally, in her estimation, to spend his money for her amusement. I should explain, of course, that I am Julia's godfather and had experienced her whims from the font to the finishing school.

So I said: "What on earth, Julia," not having thought out what I have just written first—I put that down afterwards—but because unless you know Julia you have to have at once some explanation of her. Miss Ponsonby-Stillwell, a spinster lady, sometimes misjudged her, I have noticed.

But instead of her telling me anything coherent, which after all, I did not really at the moment expect, she burst into tears. Now I have known Julia almost as long as it was possible to know so young a person and the one thing about her that had been a great comfort to me had been the fact that while she might burst into rooms, she never burst into tears.

I was so disturbed by the unexpectedness of this that I gave Evans a look, which he correctly interpreted, for he coughed slightly and left the room. I did not like the idea of a Gorland-Birmingham weeping in public, if one may grant that Evans is the public—he is a representative of it, at least, and in spite of his excellent training has certain conventional opinions that are very like those I read in one of the daily papers.

Evans' departure and my next question actually occupied only six seconds, instead of the three paragraphs in which they are here recorded. I know I am confusing two different quantities, seconds and paragraphs, but by now Julia's weeping had quite upset me. One is more sensitive, I find, just before dinner.

I pushed aside the manuscript I had been working upon, the seventh chapter of my second volume on *The Philosophy of Human Nature*, a work that had occupied my attention for many years, and I fear I left a sentence unfinished that I shall never clear up satisfactorily.

Julia said: "Something terrible has happened, Uncle Howard has been killed."

I started half way to my feet, then recovered myself.

"My poor child," I murmured, as I reached for her hand, which she gave me and sank herself on to my lap, while she dried her eyes with a little scrap of lace she called a handkerchief. I remember distinctly the glow of the light from my desk lamp on her copper-colored hair and the dainty fragrance that always clung about her person.

"A motor accident?" I asked feebly, not knowing what to say. How can one console the young in their first great grief? Inwardly I was wondering what Julia would do with all of Uncle Howard's millions, for I knew the contents of his will. There were no other relatives, as I believe I have mentioned. Actually, you know, this dialogue was moving very swiftly, but it refuses to write itself like that. Publishers who had considered my plans for my philosophy have already warned me about this. And, of course, I felt bad about Uncle Howard, too. We had been classmates at college and life-long friends ever since—you know what that means.

"Cousin Robert," Julia said impressively, and I was impressed because that term is reserved only for her solemn moments, otherwise I am merely Bobbie to her, "Cousin Robert, Uncle Howard has been murdered."

I could not think of anything to say upon this announcement, because, after all, the experience was totally new to me. I could not recall a single case of one of our crowd who had been murdered. Anyway, why had this happened? Who could possibly want to kill Howard Birmingham, one of the kindliest and most philanthropic of men, whose purse was always at the disposal of any good cause?

"Mu-murdered?" I stammered, "When?"

"Just now—before I came here," Julia went on, "in my dressing room—stabbed with a little knife from—from my own manicure set—I was downstairs—alone—arranging some flowers—and when I went upstairs to my room—to finish dressing—I found him."

"And you've notified the police?" I cried.

"Not yet—I came straight here to you, Cousin Robert—what else was there to do—and—and—"

"Good heavens!" I gasped, pushing her to her feet and reaching for the telephone on my desk. "Every second may be precious if we are to catch the murderer."

"I didn't notify the police," said Julia quietly, "because they will think I did it. That was why I came to you instead."

For some reason that I could not at the instant analyze, my hand that was reaching for the telephone paused. There was a look in Julia's glorious blue-eyes that frightened me.

"But anyone may go into your room and find him now, while we are here talking—"

"I locked the door—here is the only key to my dressing room, and it is Eloise's day out. Uncle Howard sent the other servants out, too, for we were going to the Ritz for dinner. Said we would let ourselves in when we got back."

"Do you mean you were alone in the house when this happened?"

"Yes, Cousin Robert, I was downstairs, I tell you, arranging some flowers—for Uncle Howard's desk."

"And you heard nothing? Saw no one?"

"Not a sound, not a soul, until I found him dead," and the tears rolled down Julia's face again.

"When did you find him?"

"At six-thirty-three. I remembered what you are always saying about time and looked at my watch. I came here at once in a taxi."

"Good girl," I said, making a note of six thirty-three. "Let us compare watches."

She held out her slender arm and I matched the jewelled platinum wrist watch with my own Swiss chronometer. Her watch was inaccurate by only two and three-fifths seconds. I made a note also of this.

"For all ordinary purposes, your watch is right," I said.

"You don't know, Cousin Robert—what a dreadful fix I am in."

"Nonsense, little girl," I said, patting her arm which somehow I had held after comparing the watches. "No one, not even the police, could possibly accuse you of murdering your Uncle Howard—why, everyone knows you were devoted to him."

"Cousin Robert—a week ago we had a dreadful quarrel—and Eloise heard us—she knew all about it—and so did the other servants—and I have always suspected Eloise has an evil mind, but she was so clever with lingerie I've always kept her on. Good maids are so hard to find."

"Quarrel?—with your uncle? Impossible!" I cried.

"Well, we did—and you know uncle can be very stubborn."

I nodded, for indeed it was through his stubbornness and his faith in his own opinions that he had made his millions, whereas I only inherited mine, a much easier way.

"It was because I was beginning to feel sorry that I thought I would arrange some flowers for uncle's desk—when—when—this happened." Julia's lips trembled a little.

"What did you quarrel about? Surely, the police could not consider any quarrel between you two as a serious one?"

"It was about money—oh, I don't mean my bills for hats and frocks—uncle used to grumble at them but he liked to pay them because he enjoyed having me wear pretty things—"

Again I nodded, for if it had been possible to spoil Julia—which, thank heaven, it wasn't,—Uncle Howard would have done it with the reckless allowance he gave her.

"But, you see, I also owed a lot of money—to other people—"

At this, I sat up in amazement and stared at Julia. For a second, I had a vision of her as I saw her once when a little girl, holding a doll in her arms and telling me solemnly that she had been very naughty. It turned out she had taken some chocolates contrary to the instructions of her nurse. I almost smiled at the thought of Julia being naughty.

"I owed Frieda Minters an awful lot for bridge—I'm simply no good at contract. Well, you know how Uncle Howard hated gambling—it was one of his pet sermons on modern depravity—so I didn't dare tell him, hoping to pay Frieda back out of my allowance. But Frieda got nasty about being kept waiting—it really was an awful lot of money, and I was an idiot to lose it, but there, it was done and that was that—and I had to pay it back—so she suggested,—Frieda,—I mean, that I take a little flyer on a tip—"

"Take a what?" I asked, for Julia was an extremely rapid speaker and I found it difficult to marshal her facts in their correct order, particularly when so colloquially expressed.

"Stock market, Cousin Robert—stocks and shares, that sort of thing—you buy them long and sell them short, or else it's the other way around—I never could remember—there's an awful lot to it, bulls and bears, you know—ever so many details."

"Stock market, my dear Julia! What do you mean? With your allowance?"

"Yes—you see Toby said it was a sure thing—"

"Toby?" I interrupted, for the nickname, or whatever it was, was new to me.

"You wouldn't know," Julia suddenly hesitated, then continued: "Margins or something that was going up—Frieda advised it, too—only the consolidation didn't come off and Toby explained it was unforeseen and the margins were wiped out—and then I owed thousands—because there had been lots of margins, only I hadn't paid for them—Toby said he would carry me—but in the end, of course, he had to have his money. I tried to get it from uncle, although it was a staggering sum and I couldn't explain why I needed it—not with uncle's views on gambling, for that was what it was, even if Toby did think it investing at first—and that was the row—I asked uncle for one hundred and fifty thousand dollars and couldn't explain. I tried to lie about a hospital, but he tripped me up at once—you know how shrewd uncle was—and that made it worse. I refused to tell him what I wanted the money for."

"My dear child," I gasped, staggered. Never had I heard such a story outside the pages of these periodicals I keep by my bedside for relaxation from philosophy.

"The important question is who is Toby," I said at last, when I had in part recovered my breath.

"That's what I've been thinking," said Julia, pursing her lips. "You see, he has already threatened me because I haven't paid."

"Threatened you?"

"Yes. Blackmail, I suppose. Told me if I didn't pay, he was ruined,—and in that case, he would tell a pretty dirty story about my share in it."

"Give me his address," I cried. "I'll send him a check in the morning."

"That will be too late. He gave me until midnight tonight, Cousin Robert."

"Midnight? For God's sake, is this a melodrama?"

"I think it is, Cousin Robert. At any rate, my reputation seems rather involved."

I stood up, for I have sometimes found I can collect my thoughts by pacing up and down the room. Evans entered.

"Dinner has been waiting fifteen minutes, sir," he said in as near a tone of reproach as he thought it fit to allow himself.

"I am not dining to-night, Evans," I replied.

"No, sir. Very good, sir," and the reproachful tone was re-enforced by a similar look.

"And you may telephone the Gordon Trues that—er—business—no—that won't do—they know I have no business except my book on philosophy—"

"Quite so, sir," said Evans with unnecessary agreement.

"That I have been unaccountably detained from joining them. You may emphasize the word 'unaccountably.'"

"Thank you, sir," said Evans, and left the room.

"And that brings me back again," I remarked from the mantel where I had paused to check the French clock with my Swiss chronometer—"to who is Toby?"

"That's only his nickname," said Julia, who had consulted the little mirror in her vanity case during Evans' brief appearance, "He's known as Dudley Flurrel, but we called him Toby because Dud didn't sound polite."

I picked up the social register.

"Dudley Flurrel—F-l-u-r-r-e-l?" I asked, turning to the Fs.

"Yes, but you won't find him there—I've looked already," said Julia. "And you won't find him listed or known to the brokerage house to which he said he belonged—Gay, Marshall and Penrose—

because I've asked all three of them—Tubby Gay, Sid Marshall and Babe Penrose in person—and they didn't lose my money because they never heard of Toby."

"Who introduced you to this person?"

"Frieda Minters. He was one of her gardenia and bridge gang. Frieda is fearfully upset that he turned out to be someone nobody knows—although I didn't dare tell her about the threat. Blackmail is always confidential, isn't it?"

"I believe so," I said, while I turned over in my mind Julia's latest information. Could she in her innocence have walked into a trap set by professional criminals? I began to believe so, repugnant as the thought was to my mind.

"Well," said Julia suddenly, with a new note in her voice, "I thought if anyone could get me out of this, Cousin Robert could— with all his knowledge of philosophy. But what shall we do about uncle?"

"Uncle?" I asked with a start, for my thoughts had been working on Toby.

"Uncle Howard. He is lying dead in my dressing room and nobody but you and me know."

"And the person who killed him," I corrected her.

"I'd forgotten that," said Julia. "Does that mean more blackmail?"

I found this thought a peculiarly disturbing one. Just what was the web that had been woven about Julia?

"You said you must pay this money before midnight?"

"Yes."

"Where?"

"Done up in a package—cash—to the headwaiter at the Garden of Aphrodite."

"The Garden of Aphrodite? Bless my soul."

"Oh, that's only a night club in the west Fifties, Bobbie. Don't you remember? I took you there once and you said afterwards the bill was all out of proportion? Of course it was—that was the fun of it."

I confess I do not always see eye to eye with Julia's sense of humor.

"One hundred and fifty thousand dollars in cash—in a package—to be handed to a headwaiter!"

"That was what Toby said. And he said it rather nastily."

"And you have no idea where Toby lives?"

"Not the vaguest. He used to hint about a penthouse on Park Avenue—but nothing specific."

"Do you think we should have the money, as directed?"

"You should have heard what Toby said when I said it wasn't possible. You'll produce the money or I'll make the dirtiest scandal this town has known yet."

"That would be a large threat."

"It was—for I saw then by the look in his eyes that he was a crook. Oh, how could Frieda and I have our legs pulled by a person like that?"

"He hasn't tried to blackmail Frieda?"

"No—at least, she wouldn't be likely to tell me, would she?"

"It is now seven thirty one," I said, "and we have until midnight. I'll call Beeson Smith on the telephone."

"What for?"

"To lend me a package of one hundred and fifty thousand dollars in cash," I replied. "Beeson Smith is a person with resources material and mental. He will do it for me without affecting surprise or being impertinently curious."

I took down the receiver and called a certain number. When the familiar voice of my friend replied, I stated briefly my desire for the cash, as described, to be delivered immediately at my apartment, there to be placed in the hands of Evans in case of my temporary absence.

"I told you to leave Consolidated Borax alone," was his only comment, after promising to deliver the cash within thirty minutes. I left him for obvious reasons under the misapprehension of his insinuation.

I might add, by way of explanation, that Beeson Smith was reputed to make a great deal of money by keeping on hand in a vault in his house, a large sum of ready cash to lend in those emergencies in which even important operators on the exchange sometimes find themselves. I should pay, I knew, a tidy price for the cash, even though I planned to return the loan as soon as my bank opened in the morning. But one cannot expect such favors as Beeson Smith could dispense without paying handsomely for the service.

"Now come," I said to Julia. "We must go back to your uncle's house."

"Yes, I suppose we must," she said with a shudder, and her eyes filled again.

I touched a bell and Evans entered.

"The car, Evans—the Packard will do—and I am expecting a package containing a large sum of money—one hundred and fifty thousand dollars, to be exact."

"Yes, sir."

"Sign the receipt for it and put the package in my wall safe."

"Very good, sir. Martin is already outside with the Packard, sir. He was expecting to take you on to the theatre, you recall, sir."

"Ah, so he was.—Come along, Julia."

We paused for a moment in the glare and rush of the New York street while the doorman summoned my car to the curb. Somewhere beneath the roar of the traffic and the flashing lights of the electric signs was hidden the murderer of Howard Birmingham as well as the thief and blackmailer of Julia. Were they one and the same man, or was it a gang of crooks combining, for reasons of their own, a murder with a hold-up?

They were difficult questions to be thrust upon a philosopher at the age of forty-five, and the only step I had decided upon for the moment was not to notify the police until I was certain I could clear Julia's skirts from all the threatened stains. "After all," I reflected, as I helped Julia into my car, "we have plenty of money—and that is probably a greater power than the crooks can summon to their aid."

## II
## THE HOUSE IN THE EAST EIGHTIES

"NOT A STAIN shall cling to your skirts," I murmured as I sat beside Julia. I was in reality thinking and unaware I had spoken aloud.

"It would be more to the point," remarked Julia, "if you could invent a way of keeping them off my stockings," and she innocently extended a stretch of silk hosiery that began with the daintiest of insteps and continued, *allegro ma non troppo* as it were, to a goodish distance above the knee. I am continually forgetting the change in women's fashions. In my youth, I reflected, legs were forbidden fruit and although it still required an effort on my part to regard them with complete detachment so to speak, I was not above thanking the gods of Paris that had summoned them into view. She pointed to a tiny spot of mud on her calf.

"Give me your handkerchief, Bobbie," she said, reaching into my pocket, and having procured my best Madras silk print, proceeded to scrub the mud spot with it. I might add, by way of apology for having a printed silk handkerchief with evening clothes, that I had absentmindedly put on my afternoon top-coat in leaving my apartment. It was careless of Evans to let me do it, but he had been obviously upset by the sequence of events.

Martin stopped the car before the familiar old fashioned brownstone house in the east Eighties. The only change it had undergone since Howard Birmingham had first bought it had been the removal of the old flight of steps by which one had once upon a time climbed to the front door. Now one entered by what used to be called the "English basement," why, I never knew, for I never saw a house in England that had an English basement. On the same principle as "English breakfast tea," which is also a brand unknown in England, I reflected.

I told Martin to wait, and then I took the latch-key from Julia. She clung tightly to my arm as we entered the lower lobby which Howard Birmingham had had done over with onyx panelling. It looked for all the world as if it had been decorated with slabs of Castille soap. We climbed the imposing marble stairs, because I particularly dislike these automatic lifts in which you have to shut yourself as in a cage and then press the right numbered button. It is a horrible sensation to ascend in something over which one has no control.

As we came to the first floor I paused to look about. Julia had left all the lights burning.

"Show me where you were arranging the flowers," I said.

"Here in uncle's study," she answered, leading the way into a large mahogany room off the drawing room. I knew it well for Howard and I had had many a chat there about the problems of philosophy. Howard was distinctly a pragmatist. My own leaning is toward Platonism.

I glanced at the familiar built-in shelves, filled with books, which extended from floor to ceiling all around the room, except at one place which was occupied by a huge open fireplace. The shelves were lined with unbroken sets of novelists and historians in expensive bindings.

"Some day I'll have time to read 'em," Howard had said. Now that day would never come, and the volumes would remain unread.

In the centre of the room was a large flat-topped desk of carved mahogany with Howard's chair in front of it. In the middle was a vase of handsome roses, as Julia had said, and beside it a pair of clipping scissors and some scattered leaves and stems which she had not cleared away.

"Flowers were arranged," I thought to myself, bearing in mind the dictum of the philosopher Descartes to doubt all things until they could be proved. In the waste basket I found a receipted bill for roses, torn in half, a few rose petals, and the box in which the flowers had been delivered. Nothing else.

There were no papers lying loosely about on Howard's desk. He was one of those men who prided himself on not leaving his seat until his desk was clear. All was in the fanatically neat order on which he set such store. I wondered a bit about fingerprints and decided for the present to touch nothing in the room.

I think we paused in Howard's study two or three minutes longer than necessary, for we were both reluctant to climb to what waited for us on the floor above. At last, however, I strode up the stairs, a less gorgeous flight than that from the floor below, but still of cursedly slippery marble, and Julia followed, with one hand clinging fast to the coat tail of my evening suit. I stared at the wall on one side and at the bannisters on the other as if expecting to see somewhere a clue, but this house was too immaculate to make the idea plausible.

Before the door at which Julia nodded I stopped while she handed me another key, a little flat silver thing that fitted into an intricate looking lock. Why is it one always tries first to turn a flat key in the wrong direction?

"The other way, Bobbie," I heard Julia say, and then I noticed that my hand was shaking slightly.

The door opened and I stared into blank darkness.

"I'm so sorry," said Julia, "I switched this light off when I left."

I saw her reach around the side of the door and as a button clicked the room was flooded with light.

Howard was lying on his back with his mouth open—I recall distinctly how ghastly he looked with his teeth gleaming and that set expression upon his face and then I saw his evening dress shirt bosom stained with blood, and lying in a pool of blood almost under his arm, a shining manicure knife, a sort of lancet-like affair, with a chased silver handle. He wore no coat but was otherwise dressed for dinner.

Julia was leaning heavily against me now but I was hardly conscious of it—only afterwards did I recall the weight of her warm, slender body against my side. As I bent over Howard's body I could hear the ticking of his watch in his waistcoat pocket.

"There was no struggle then," I thought to myself, "at least, not a violent one, or the watch would not be ticking still."

Then I looked around the room and its neat appearance confirmed my impression that there had been no anticipated attack and consequent resistance. Everything was in order, except for one or two of Julia's intimate garments flung across a chair and her toilet articles open upon her dressing table. I noted that the other pieces of her manicure set matched the knife upon the floor.

"How were the windows?" I asked.

"Locked," I heard Julia whisper, "and on the inside. I looked at once."

I walked over to the windows and confirmed this. I peered cautiously through the heavy hangings and saw only the blank wall of the opposite house across a light well. It was too dark to see down into the unlighted area below. I felt certain, however, that even Edgar Allan Poe's great ape could not have climbed up or down that blank wall, but he might have used a ladder, I thought, if there were any way of getting one into the light well.

"What is down there?" I asked Julia, pointing at the windows.

"Nothing," she replied. "Our house and the next are built around all four sides, and the house opposite has no windows on the air space. The owner said he didn't care to have neighbors spying on him and bricked them all up."

"Man differs from a dog," I recalled a fellow philosopher saying once, "in that a dog never looks up. His horizon is bounded by the level of his eyes and below, but includes nothing over his head, unless special effort is made to attract his attention upwards."

I decided to look upwards out the window. Very cautiously I opened half the casement of the left hand window and peered upward. Again I saw only blank wall above on all sides, and some stars twinkling overhead. There was enough glow from the city sky for me to make out the walls dimly. I brought my head back inside, closed and locked the casement again, and carefully arranged the hangings to blot out all light from within.

"Do you think you have left your fingerprints on the window fastenings?" I heard Julia ask.

I started in dismay at my stupidity, for I may have obliterated others, however innocent my own.

"Did you leave your windows locked and the curtains drawn when you went down to attend to the flowers?" When embarrassed, ask an important sounding question.

"Yes, of course. I had just been getting into my evening gown, as you can see," and she indicated with a nod the pink and lace things on the chair.

"And where does this door lead to?" I asked, indicating one of two doors in the wall opposite the entrance from the hall passage.

"To Uncle Howard's rooms at the back, and this one," she replied, pointing to the one further away from the windows, "to my bathroom and my bedroom beyond."

"A singularly deep house," I commented, putting on my gloves to avoid any further accidental confusion of fingerprints.

"Uncle's rooms were built out in a new extension at the back," Julia explained. "He has his own staircase down to a hallway leading to his study. Naturally, he didn't have to come through my dressing room to get in and out of his own quarters."

"May I look into your bedroom?"

"Of course, you funny old fogey," and Julia almost giggled, in spite of what lay on the floor before us.

I managed to turn the handle of the door by reaching behind the knob, so as not to destroy any evidence on its gleaming surface and looked in. Again Julia touched a switch and lighted up the room. There was evidence that Julia had recently taken a bath, probably before dressing to go down to arrange the flowers. Her afternoon dress was in a heap on the floor as well as some stockings and a pair of mules. A bath towel, still damp, was crumpled in a corner. I crossed the room to the bedroom door and looked in there. On either side of an antique four-poster bed, hung with chintz curtains, were windows over which the hangings were also drawn and the casements locked.

So far I had seen not a single scrap of evidence or a clue of any kind and I began to feel that the task of a detective was more difficult than I had imagined. I had been told by persons supposed to know that there was always something. But the three rooms all spoke so intimately of Julia and of nothing else, save for the body lying in the pool of blood on the rug before her dressing table.

I came back to the door leading to Howard Birmingham's rooms.

"Let us look in there, too, my dear," I said. She followed me along the hall until we came to the door.

"That is uncle's bedroom," she said.

I found the door was locked.

"He must have the key on him," Julia suggested. "He always locked his room when he went out, but in that case, why didn't he put on his coat?"

"We can form no theory because we have not yet got all our facts straight," I replied, trying to sound wise, but in reality I was beginning to be worried by the mystery.

"We mustn't be too long, because Eloise may come home early," Julia intervened, as I stood baffled before the locked door.

"Eloise?"

"My maid—the one with the afternoon off. She has a shrewd face with an unpleasant expression around the mouth sometimes. The chef says she has a rotten temper. But she was always nice enough to me—I gave her lots of my dresses and things—undies and the like—so she never showed her temper, if she has one, to me."

"Eloise certainly must not walk in on us," I replied, and returned hastily to the dressing room. There I closed and locked the door on the inside. My watch showed that we had so far spent forty-eight minutes and twenty-nine seconds on our inspection of the house.

"When will the other servants be likely to return?" I asked.

"Probably not until late."

"How many are there."

"Achille, the chef; Mary O'Brien, the kitchen girl, who is also the vegetable cook; William Gasple, the dishwasher and handy man, and Grierson, the butler, and his footman, Tony Salvatore; the two parlor maids, Ellen Butler and Sarah Niehr; the house-maid, Fanny Carroll, and the chauffeur who sleeps out—besides Eloise."

"That makes nine and a possible ten, if the chauffeur does turn up."

"Right, Bobbie."

"We might as well be standing at the information desk at the Grand Central," I remarked, looking down at Howard.

"But, of course, you have thought of something, Bobbie! Look how easily you got the hundred and fifty thousand dollars for me."

"Yes," I replied. "I have thought of one thing. Your Uncle Howard has got to die a natural death—at least for the time being—and we've got to have a doctor who will certify it."

My reason for this announcement was to gain time. There was the matter of the hundred and fifty thousand dollars to be delivered by midnight, and to call the police in now would jeopardize Julia's connection with the blackmailer. He might act at once, believing that we had called in the police against him. The horrible words "accessory after the fact" kept ringing in my ears, but until the other matter of the attempted blackmailing of Julia was settled, I could think of nothing else to do. Even criminals, I knew, had trouble in disposing of a murdered man, to say nothing of a philosopher, who would normally be lacking in any knowledge of the technique.

"But Bobbie, we must find the murderer."

"Yes," I replied, "but not tonight. For tonight, it is a natural death. Don't forget the Garden of Aphrodite."

"I haven't," replied Julia, "and I've been wondering if we have time for everything."

"At least, we can try," I said, looking at my watch. "If only I knew a doctor who was a specialist at his job as Beeson Smith is at his."

"Didn't you help Tommy Billingworth through medical school—and make me dance with him once or twice afterwards, although he acts and looks like something in a dime museum?"

"Yes," I replied, not meaning an acquiescence in all Julia had said.

"Well, send for him. He will have to do it. I'll make him. He's a regular doctor now, isn't he?"

"Oh, yes, quite legal," I said, "only he is one of these people with a conscience: his father was a saloonkeeper and gave his son a strict bringing up. Besides, if anything comes out, it will blast his career."

"Rot," exclaimed Julia. "Leave him to me, and it's up to you, Bobbie, to see that nothing comes out."

What was it the poet said about how hopelessly involved one gets when first one practices to deceive? But I banished the thought, for I felt now past any half measures.

Julia and I carefully let ourselves out, locked the door once more on the outside, and returned to the study on the floor below where there was a telephone on Howard's desk. "One thing I am certain of, Julia."

"What is that?" she asked, as she turned over the pages of the telephone directory to look up Tommy Billingworth's number. My eyes are not so good as they were.

"That this thing was an inside job."

"You mean, it was done by someone already in the house?" and I noticed that she paused for a moment and turned one or two pages without looking at them.

"Yes," I replied. "At what time did Eloise leave?"

"I don't know exactly, because after I dismissed her she went upstairs to dress. I told her I was through with her at lunch-time."

"And the others?"

"Uncle Howard told them they could all go as soon as they could make it—he often said that to the servants when we were dining out—even dismissed the chauffeur and said we would go in a taxi. He had some funny notions about democracy and in his heart always resented a butler—even as perfect a one as Grierson. He loved to have an afternoon off now and then without servants."

"And you don't know when they went?"

"Not all of them together, of course. But I went around to Frieda Minters soon after luncheon, to see if she knew anything more about Toby—you see, I had this midnight date hanging over me, and at the last moment, say after dinner, I was going to appeal to you anyway—and that made me think I had rowed with uncle about nothing after all—for I knew you would lend me the money—so I stopped in at the florists' to order some roses to prove I was sorry—and when I got back, they had come and uncle had paid for them, although I meant to and forgot, so they came C.O.D., because I got them at a strange shop—and then I went up and took a bath and when I was dressed, I went down to arrange the flowers and the rest you know. There were no servants in the house when I got back—oh, here's Tommy's number, under the Bs," and she read it off.

I spoke a few words over the telephone and within ten minutes, in eight minutes and thirty-five seconds to be accurate, Tommy rang the front door bell, as a taxi moved away, and Julia and I let him in at once. We had been waiting close to the front door in order to observe if any of the servants were going to turn up first.

I made Tommy sit down in a leather arm chair in Howard's study and I gave him one of Howard's corona coronas from a box on the table. Tommy handled it gingerly as if it were a high explosive. I could see now what Julia meant. He brushed his hair, which was black and oily, but also thin, straight back from his sharp, hatchet face. On the top of an enormous nose he perched a pair of shell goggles, each lens of which was almost as large as the porthole in a ship. His clothes also looked black and oily and his cravat was apparently mounted on ball bearings, for it slid from ear to ear and seldom rested in the center. Its migrations still further emphasized the flexibility of his Adam's apple which rose and fell, when he talked, above a collar that opened unexpectedly between two white wings to expose this portion of his neck. I did not feel so kindly disposed toward him as I had when he was a gawky youth whose way I had paid through college. Why are the fruits of philanthropy so rarely aesthetic in appearance?

And yet I blessed his conscience for one quality: I knew that if I made him swear not to reveal what I was about to tell him, no torture could extract it from him. On the other hand, I was extremely uncertain that he would help. There is a difference between silence and action.

As tactfully and as rapidly as I could, for time was getting on and servants and the Garden of Aphrodite were looming over our heads, I laid the situation before Tommy, together with a request for a certificate of death from natural causes, either heart failure or apoplexy, whichever he preferred.

When I made an end of my eloquence, Tommy squirmed in his chair and ruined half of the corona corona.

"Why not wish this job on his regular physician?" he asked in a tone of voice I did not like.

I kicked Julia on the shin and blessed the short skirt that made this feat more effective. She was about to make what I felt would be a tactless remark.

"You know old Dr. Spargill as well as I do," I said. "Can you imagine him doing anything unethical? Or in fact, doing anything except feeling a pulse, shaking his head, and offering a choice between calomel and cod liver oil?"

Fortunately for us, there was an interruption. A footstep came softly along the passage and I saw standing at the door a rather pertly pretty looking woman with a hard expression around the mouth.

"Eloise!" exclaimed Julia.

"Yes, miss. I've just got in. Is there anything I can do for you, miss?" Eloise asked, looking sharply, I thought, from me to Tommy.

Julia silenced my half-opened mouth by saying:

"Eloise, something terrible has happened. The master—Mr. Birmingham—had a fatal stroke this afternoon. This is Dr. Billingworth whom Mr. Cornua"—(I forgot to mention that my name is Robert Cornua)—"called in in the emergency. Dr. Spargill could not be reached."

I marveled at Julia's glibness.

"How dreadful, miss," said Eloise, but it struck me at the time that although the tone of her voice sounded appropriate, she did not appear to be surprised. "I'm so sorry, miss. Can I help you in any way?"

"No, thank you. Yes—you might sit up in the servants' hall until the others come in so they won't come bothering us here. You may tell them the news, of course. Mr. Robert is taking charge, as Mr. Birmingham's closest friend."

"Certainly, miss," said Eloise, but I distrusted her eye and her expression. "Is—is the master in—in his room?" she asked.

"No—in mine," said Julia. "It happened there. Please don't have anyone come knocking on doors."

"Of course not," replied the maid. She looked me over rather coolly, I thought, as she turned and left the room.

"I suppose you know that we shall have to have an accommodating undertaker, too, don't you?" said Tommy Billingworth.

"An accommodating undertaker?" I asked blankly.

"Well, if my certificate reads apoplexy in technical language, and the undertaker finds a knife wound, he will need to be accommodating—and such accommodation, I understand, is expensive."

"Money is no object," I replied sharply.

"Tommy, don't make difficulties now you've agreed to be nice," said Julia.

"Pardon me, but I didn't make this difficulty. It is inherent in the problem, which Mr. Cornua will understand because he is a philosopher. And if I have agreed to my part, it is because I couldn't very well help it. But I tell you I don't like it. Nothing good comes of lies, and if I had known what I was getting into, you can bet I wouldn't have come."

"That's all very moral and fine, but we've got to be practical," said Julia.

"Yes," I said. "I've explained to you the situation. Now about this undertaker."

"Well, if we all fry in the electric chair, don't say I didn't warn you," said Tommy gloomily.

"I think you are vulgar," said Julia.

"Well," agreed Tommy, "I guess I am—and so's the most of the world—and they are the guys to look out for. A spade is a spade and a murder is a murder, and I don't see why we don't call in the police and go to it."

"I've told you why we can't," I exclaimed with annoyance. Time was running on.

"And I don't like the look of your maid, Julia—"

"Miss Gorland, if you please," cut in Julia sharply. A pessimist is so quickly unpopular.

"Miss Gorland, then. If that girl ain't a natural born detective, I'm the emperor of China. She's going to be another expensive item in the bill before we're through. She smelt fish the first shot out of the box."

"Must you be so vulgar?" Julia remarked.

"The undertaker," I said firmly.

"How high will you go?" asked Tommy, reaching for the telephone book.

"Anything in reason," I answered.

"This ain't a reasonable proposition," he said. "It's got to be more than that."

"Fix your own terms."

"No—he'll fix his," said Tommy, and took down the receiver.

"This Joe Smats?" he asked, after some parleying with central over the number. "Say, listen, Joe. This is Tom Billingworth talking—yeah, Tom—you know. No, I don't want any more stiffs—at least, not tonight. I got one for you. Sure—that's right—only, it's a kind of special case. Now wait a minute, Joe—there's money in it— real money—the kind you dream about. Yeah, it's that kind of case. You just get paid for saying nothing—see? Now listen, Joe, it's strictly O.K. but it can't be public, see? I'm fixing up the certificate—there's nothing to it—just a little private affair—no, Joe—no gunmen—nothing like that. It's a swell party, see? No front page tabloid stuff, get me? That's what we are avoiding, see? And it's worth a bunch of kale to choke it off, see? Listen, Joe, I guarantee it's on the level. . . . Sure, I'm in it . . . It's just one of them things . . . we can't spill it, that's all. Good and sufficient reasons, get me? It would be a big noise, see? and they won't stand for it—Park Avenue stuff. They'll pay anything—get me? Anything to keep it on the Q.T. . . . No politics, I promise that. No, not a chanct of a comeback—nothing political—you don't risk a thing. Write your own check—oh, all right, cash then. Just name it, and they'll send it in a truck if you can't carry it away. Sure. . . . Well, I'm risking that, too. . . . What's that? I'm not married? What of it? I'm offering you Santa Claus for the wife and kiddies—sure—for life. . . . You will? . . . Say, Joe, that's a lot of money—oh, all right—hold on, Joe. We accept—sure. Spot cash when underground—how's that? O.K. Here's the address—hop in the bus and come right around. Hurry—there's a reason."

Tommy hung up the receiver and wiped his forehead with the wrong kind of silk handkerchief.

"That guy is an arguer. He wants an amendment to the Constitution before he stirs a step."

"How much?" I asked.

"Ten grand," said Tommy.

"Ten what?"

"Berries, beans, bones, shekels, Mr. Cornua—ten thousand promises printed in green on special paper to pay one dollar in lawful coin of the republic on demand—get me? Ten thousand dollars—that's all. You can't go into this kind of business on a shoestring."

"For what?" I asked with dignity.

"For complete and absolute silence."

"It's blackmail," exclaimed Julia.

"Well," said Tommy, "I wouldn't worry about names when we are getting results."

"Is this person—this Joe—reliable?"

"When you pay his price—but if you don't, oh boy!" said Tommy. "That's all you can ask of anyone, ain't it?" he went on.

## III
## THE UNDERTAKER UNDERTAKES

IN SEVENTEEN MINUTES from Tommy's last words the doorbell rang.

"Shall I answer it, Miss Julia?" we heard Eloise's voice call out from somewhere in the rear of the house.

"No, thank you," replied Julia.

"Better let me," said Tommy, pushing past me. "He might take a suspicion to you."

The door was opened and Mr. Joe Smats crossed the threshold. Although he was dressed in the lugubrious black of his profession, I was unfavorably impressed by the decided aroma of alcohol that permeated the atmosphere about him like an aura.

"I've told the boys to wait outside until ready," said Mr. Smats, offering me a dirty and greasy hand to shake. "Just show me the way."

"I think, Julia," I whispered aside to her, "that you had better wait in the study."

She hesitated a moment, and then nodded.

Tommy Billingworth and Joe Smats followed me upstairs to the door of Julia's dressing-room which I unlocked.

"I'm asking no question so you don't need to say a word," said Joe Smats reassuringly to me as we mounted the stairs.

We entered the room.

"Just what I figured it was," said Joe Smats, looking down at the corpse and sucking an ivory tooth pick as he did so. "But I'll stick to my word and no question asked. That's me. You know me, Doc. Fifteen years on the job and never spilled a bean—not for a friend, at any rate," and he looked me over rather coolly. He turned back to Howard's body.

"Didn't want to make a noise," said Mr. Smats picking up the manicure knife and looking at it closely. "Must have been somebody else in the house at the time. How come he let them sneak up on him?—no place to hide here, except back of them curtains in the bathroom." He went on looking around the room. "Husky guy like him ought to of put up a fight—middle aged, but no push over at that."

Mr. Smats' eyes continued to search the room.

"Well, I'm a son of a gun," he said as his eyes travelled over the dressing table. "This dinky little knife is out of the manicure set. So that's why they elected us, eh Tom?" and Mr. Smats' eyes fixed themselves on me again.

"You'll have to make it heart failure, Tom, so we can lay him out in his own bed and doctor up this knife cut," said Mr. Smats making play upon some gold bridgework with his ivory tooth pick. "It's a damned lucky thing it's small and clean," he went on as he knelt beside the body and opened the shirt. "We'll just have to undress him, burn the clothes, wash the wound, plug it up with beeswax and a little make-up, and no one will never know the difference. Then when you've signed your certificate, Tom, I can take it away. I don't suppose the family physician will come butting in?"

"I'm certain I can prevent that," I replied. "My friend Archie Newsome is now at Miami, I'll wire him to send for Dr. Spargill tonight—order a special train—and ship him off, you know."

"Your friend at Miami will come through with his telegram?"

"Certainly. He will understand that my reason must be important. He will not question it."

"Say, Tom, there must be some stuff in this high society dope called 'good form' that we haven't figured on. We can't get our little gun boys trained like that. They have to have just one reason—the coin."

Mr. Smats began to whistle a cheerful tune—I believe it is called "Wake Up and Dream"—while he busied himself about Howard's body, emptying the pockets of the trousers with what appeared like extreme dexterity. But I noticed that he put on a pair of thin rubber gloves before he touched anything.

"Keys," said Mr. Smats tossing me a bunch on a ring. "Four hundred and fifty-six dollars and eighty-five cents in loose change—I'll just keep it—I may have to scatter a little chicken feed around if there's any hitch. Watch—gold—about five hundred dollars new, but there's nothing in this Swiss stuff—who'll pay its value?—Hullo, picture inside the case—looks like the Jane downstairs."

"Her mother!" I exclaimed involuntarily in my surprise, as I peered over Mr. Smats' shoulder.

Why, I wondered to myself, did the case of Howard Birmingham's watch contain a picture of Julia's mother—the sister of Mrs. Howard Birmingham—instead of that of his own wife? I was glad Julia had not come upstairs.

"I'll take the watch, if you please," I said to Smats.

"O. K. by me," he remarked handing it over.

I opened the case and stared at the little photograph. There was no doubt about it—the picture was that of Julia's mother. I slipped it out and turned it over. On the back I found written "Always—Amy." Amy was the name of Julia's mother. I put the photograph away in my bill folder, an act which did not escape the observant eyes of Mr. Smats.

"Of course," he said in a casual tone of voice, "I'm being paid just to keep quiet—but take a tip from me, mister, you are salting away in your pocketbook something that'll land you up the river—this is my professional advice, that's all. But don't forget that a photograph always means three people—the guy who took the picture, the picturee, and the person who owns it. You can't shake 'em all off."

"Two of them are dead," I said.

"That leaves only one—the guy who took the picture—it's no amateur snapshot—I could see the head had been cut out of one of these swell studio pictures—which means it can be traced. I'm just telling you for your own good. It's not my funeral."

"It is a chance I must take," I answered.

Mr. Smats shrugged and resumed his whistling.

"Here's a lodge pin," he remarked as he slipped off Howard's waistcoat.

"College fraternity," I corrected Mr. Smats, and showed him that I also wore one like it. I thought he might trust my motives more if he saw that Howard and I were fraternity brothers.

"Well, I'll say you've lived up to all the bylaws of your crime club, if you ask me."

"You have observed," I said, "that robbery was not the motive for this killing. Nothing has been taken."

"Say, mister, I'm not feeble-minded just because I can't afford to eat at the Ritz. There's three reasons why somebody in this house—sure, it's an amateur job, but neat—pretty lucky, that part of it—only one of three reasons why this old bird got bumped off. One, somebody is going to inherit his money and needs it now"—I started, I could not help myself—but of course, the idea was absurd, preposterous—"two, somebody has something on him and he wouldn't come across," Mr. Smats continued, with I could see a mental note of my start, "or three, he got in wrong with a woman some time ago and it's just come through."

"Have you any other conclusions that may help us later to find the murderer?" I asked.

"Don't make me laugh, mister. You keep on putting evidence away in your pockets and they'll find someone they can dress up for the murderer all right, all right. But yes, if you want to know—I can tell you some more."

"What?" I queried eagerly.

"Go ahead—tell him," said Tommy, who had up until now been examining and cleaning the wound. "Mr. Cornua means what he says—you can see he's only a novice."

"I said it was an amateur job—and it is—which narrows your field a lot. How do I know? The person didn't intend to kill him because the person brought no weapon along—it was impulse—the spur of the moment—not premeditated—get me? Second, no professional would trust a little manicure knife like that—why, the darned thing might have broken short off—it's light and flimsy—and spoiled the whole business. Only ignorance backed by rage, strength and luck would have driven that thin knife through a stiff shirt bosom and into this guy's heart. If it had struck a shirt stud, or a suspender buckle, or a rib, nothing much would have happened to this man—and no professional would have taken that chance."

"Have you formed any more precise theory—One pointing to individuals?" I ventured.

"Sure—you got the choice of three motives—and we got three prospects. Number one is the baby doll downstairs, all eyes and knees, number two is you, mister, the old lodge pal, who is the most likely to have something on a friend and who put away the photograph—well, you asked me, didn't you? Then let me finish; somebody on the outside working on someone inside because of a score to be paid off. Now I've seen two of you and I've no choice, but I haven't seen the third possibility—and if there's no such animal, why then you two, the little pippin downstairs and you, mister, can match to see who's it. I don't have to have a theory."

"Do you know the Garden of Aphrodite?" I asked, thinking it tactful for the present to ignore the grossness of his insinuations.

"Have I ever said 'pleased to meetcha' to Times Square," replied Mr. Smats with what I assumed was elaborate sarcasm.

"Do you know a person known as Dudley Flurrel—also called Toby—who may go there?"

"Now you're trying to get something for nothing, Mr. Cornua. Naughty-naughty," and Mr. Smats grinned and wagged a finger at me.

"Can you give me information if I pay for it?"

"Sure—I'll bring you one of the seals from the Aquarium if you'll pay for it on delivery."

"Tom—how far can I trust this man!" I asked.

"As far as you can pay him," replied Tommy. "I met him first when I was riding an ambulance and he helped me, a kid, out of my first mistake. I croaked a bird in my nervousness, gave the wrong stuff in an emergency case, and Joe here squared me with the police sergeant. The reporters never knew. Since then I've heard a lot about him—he's known as Honest Joe, the square mortician, from the Bronx to Westchester. They say half the underground wires in New York run into Joe's cellar. A responsible man like that can't take chances double-crossing the crowd he works for. He averages a job a day that's strictly confidential. Tell him what you want to know and he'll name his price. If you get together after that, Joe will come through."

Mr. Smats took this tribute to his character with an air of pleased pride.

"What will you charge for giving me precise information about a young man known as Dudley Flurrel, also called Toby, and the headwaiter at the Garden of Aphrodite—and about any others who may be associated with them?"

"It's lucky you came to me," said Mr. Smats, thoughtfully tapping the body of Howard Birmingham with his toe, "if this case is a job belonging to the gang that hangs out at the Garden. I can't figure that, though, because they're all professionals and this is amateur work. Well, you and I, Mr. Cornua, are probably going to do a lot of business together before we get through with this, so I'll give you special rates. We got to play careful because if that gang gets after us, they'll sic the police on us."

Never in my life had I expected to feel fear of the police, but I could see how skillfully Julia and I were trapped, and suddenly a light dawned on me! The criminals had made it appear like an amateur job, or they would have had no convincing hold over us. The murder was a further extension of the plan to keep Julia in their power, after she had paid the hundred and fifty thousand dollars of tribute.

"You see," said Mr. Smats, "if we could get you and the little lady downstairs clear, we could use the police ourselves. But just now we're standing against the wall with our hands up—and of course, you or she may have done it, at that. I've no prejudices, Mr. Cornua, and you won't have either when you've studied philosophy as long as I have."

"Sir," I said in indignation, "I am a lifelong student of philosophy—I am writing a book on it!"

"Oh, that," said Mr. Smats contemptuously. "I mean the real thing—men and women—not a bunch of words on a page."

"Let's get back to business. Time is growing extremely short, and I must deliver a package to the headwaiter at the Garden of Aphrodite at midnight."

"You've been holding something back on me—you haven't given me all the dope," said Mr. Smats indignantly. "All right—I'm through," and he picked up his hat from a chair and turned toward the door.

I caught his arm and by pouring out Julia's story quickly, about Dudley Flurrel and his demand for one hundred and fifty thousand dollars, I made him stay.

"You know," he said chewing his ivory tooth pick, "I think it's just a coincidence. We got two jobs here—one a stick up and the other a murder. I don't believe there's any connection—one's professional, the other amateur."

"Can you do anything?"

"Sure—the professional holdup is easy. I can run that down for you in a couple of days—but you better pay the money as agreed. Don't take any chances with what they might do about the little lady downstairs—and if they should get wind of this—goodnight."

"Why?"

"Why? Why because it would be meat for their stickup game. You don't suppose they'd quit for fifteen hundred grand if they could hang this on us, do you?"

"But suppose they did do this murder, too?"

"Then all us poor sailors is going to have a rough night at sea," said Mr. Smats thoughtfully.

"You see," continued Mr. Smats, "having made this date for tonight with Baby doll downstairs, they've had her watched ever since. They seen her go to your apartment, get you and come back. They seen Tom come—and they've looked him up by now and know he's a Doc—and they seen me come and they know me. Now, I put it to you, Mr. Cornua, if you'd seen all that and put it all together you'd figure out, wouldn't you, that there was some kind of a queer smell in our cellar?"

"We might be considering what to do about the demand for the money," I ventured.

"We might, if I wasn't here," said Mr. Smats. "But they know I mean only one thing—a stiff in the house. Now they'll be trying to figure that out, if they didn't know it before. They'll see my two boys sitting in the limousine outside, and they'll know they're my body guard, so to be safe, they've probably got them covered with a machine gun in another car, just in case of accidents, and it won't do for me to go out and tip my boys off or they'd get me sure. You see, it has frightened the whole crowd when they seen you call me into this. And all this because you didn't let Tom explain things frankly to me over the phone. In a game of this kind, Mr. Cornua, the most dangerous thing you can do is to hold out on your friends. Put that down in your book."

"I'm sorry," I said.

"So'm I," replied Smats, "but I gotta stick now, because they wouldn't ever believe I'd backed out."

"Couldn't we buy them off? Money is no object."

"You can't make 'em stay bought, see? They know my being here means we've got to get rid of something important, all right—you're outside guessing—what is it? A dead body—sure. Whose? Only one person in the house who has not come in or gone out once—Howard Birmingham, millionaire, Q. E. D. Is that news worth money to 'em? Boy, I'll say it is. Remember, they already got Julia tied up. Now they've got all of us."

"What's to be done?"

"Don't I wish you knew! Well, Mr. Cornua, the only thing to do, while I stay here and do some quiet thinking, is for you to take Julia and the package to the Garden of Aphrodite, and don't stay to see the revue. Come back here. They'll let you O. K., because it's better for them to have us all in one place. After that, we'll have to figure out whether our number is coming up or what next. On the horizon, remember sits the police—and we've passed beyond explanations with them. Don't forget, while you're out, to send that old doctor off to Miami. And be sure you stand in the door so the light shines on your face when you first open it. I don't want them mistaking you for me."

I must confess that I found it difficult to control my nervousness when I went down to get Julia. To think that in a few moments in the midst of the civilization of the twentieth century and in the great city of New York that a group of people could find themselves besieged and in deadly peril, helpless to call for aid or rescue! For a wild second, I thought of dashing in the Packard to the Grand Central, to carry Julia off on the first train—anywhere to get away—leaving Tom and Mr. Smats to their fate, but I feared that it would be useless, that vengeance would overtake us and we should be worse off than to face the danger bravely, and if necessary go down fighting to the last in Julia's defence. Not a word of all this did I say to Julia as we drove to my apartment to get the package of money.

# IV
## THE GARDEN OF APHRODITE

As MARTIN DROVE THE PACKARD AWAY, I looked out the window in the rear and saw a taxi cab swing out from the opposite curb and follow. It had only the parking lights on and the interior was dark as Stygian caves. I did not dare tell Julia any of the latest developments for fear of terrifying her, and she, relieved and confident since the arrival of Tom and Mr. Smats to our assistance, chattered almost gaily and lightheartedly. After all, adventure is always a stimulant to the young, and danger but an added spice.

At my apartment, the still disapproving Evans handed me the package.

"Twice strange voices have called up, sir, to know if you were at home. They would not give any names or numbers, or leave a message."

Someone, I thought to myself, was checking up on the report sent in by the shadowers of the Birmingham house.

"Evans," I said suddenly, inspired, "you served through the war, didn't you?"

"Yes, sir."

"Do you know how to handle an automatic."

"Rather!"

"What in the world!" cried Julia.

"Be quiet, Julia. Put this automatic in your pocket, Evans, and come with us. I'll give you any further instructions later."

I took the pistol from my desk drawer.

"Pardon me for the liberty, sir, but I knew something was up, sir. It was not eating dinner and the package of money, sir. They set me thinking, sir."

I could hardly blame Evans for his commenting upon so rare a phenomenon as allowing himself the luxury of a thought.

We returned to Martin and the Packard. Across the street I saw the dark taxi cab standing.

"The Garden of Aphrodite," I said firmly to Martin, as Evans took his seat beside my chauffeur.

The taxicab followed.

It was eight minutes to twelve when we pressed our way through a dense mob of people waiting to be shown to tables. The entrance to the Garden of Aphrodite was an unimpressive narrow door, leading into a long narrow passage, congested with the noisy mob struggling to get in. Suddenly the passage ended at the entrance of a gaily decorated square room in which tables and chairs were closely packed about a small dance floor. At the far end a jazz orchestra was making indescribable noises with saxophones. In the centre of the dance floor, as we entered, a young lady in beads was oscillating in an Oriental dance as this dance is known in Manhattan.

The head waiter obviously recognized Julia and beckoned us over the protests of the other waiting couples to a table somewhat in the shadow of a column. I had thought it best to leave Evans with Martin in the car.

"Champagne, sir?" he said, as if we were ordinary customers, and scribbled rapidly on a little pad. "Caviare canapes with the champagne?"

"What you will," I replied.

"You've brought your own supplies, I see, sir," he said, referring to the package which rested in my lap. "I'll just take it out to the serving pantry, sir."

These last two remarks were made in an obviously loud tone of voice for the benefit of the couples at the next tables to ours. He picked up the package, carried it slowly and daintily by its string, and vanished through a door with it. Never had I seen one hundred and fifty thousand dollars make so strange an exit.

"Well," said Julia, "that's that."

At this moment, a youth at another table spied Julia and came over to us. The atmosphere in his vicinity was somewhat impregnated with the vapors of Scotch whiskey.

"Hello, Julia," he said. "Dance?"

"Sure, Billy—this is Cousin Robert. At the Prom last winter—New Haven," Julia whispered to me.

"Oh," I said, and watched them glide their way through the crush on the dance floor. The solo dancer had finished.

Youth, youth, I sighed to myself, and began composing inwardly a little sentimental speech, somewhat like the style of Bulwer-Lytton. With mortal peril hanging over thy head and a king's ransom just paid into the pantry, still thou must dance and have thy fling, and it is age that pays and pays and pays—or is that a quotation from Oscar Wilde, I thought?

The headwaiter returned at this point, escorting a less important menial who carried a tray with the canapes, a bucket of ice from which emerged something done up in swaddling clothes, two bottles of White Rock, some glasses, and a flask. The head waiter slipped the flask discreetly into my lap.

"Part of your supplies, sir," he said.

Come, I thought to myself, the fellow has an instinct for the theatre.

"He says it is quite correct, sir," he added in a whisper, as he leaned over to move back a vase of flowers. "You may rest quite easy in your mind, sir, for the present."

I did not like that ominous phrase "for the present."

"Do I get anything resembling a receipt?" I asked, also in a whisper.

"Bless you, sir, don't you know the age of faith is returning," said the head waiter with an impudent grin. He held a glass to the light as if scrutinizing its cleanliness.

"I trust, sir, that Mr. Howard Birmingham is enjoying his usual good health," he said, as he put the glass down very close to me.

The man's expression was impertinent but otherwise inscrutable.

"You know him?" I parried.

"He is not a customer of ours—but his niece, Miss Julia, am I correct?—is with you tonight, so I conclude there is no foundation for the rumor?"

"What rumor?"

"Of his serious illness—a stroke or the heart, I'm not certain which—I heard scraps of something at one of the tables tonight. Very important matter to Wall Street, I imagine. It was quite a relief to see Miss Julia come in—for then I knew there was nothing in it. You see, I do a bit on margins myself, in a small way, of course, and I'm always listening in for tips from our customers. You'd be surprised, sir, what one hears in the course of a twelvemonth."

"If it is of any importance to you," I said making a sudden resolve, "Mr. Birmingham was not feeling quite himself when I left him this evening, but the doctor assured me he had no reason to anticipate anything serious."

"How fortunate to have an optimist for a family physician. I am rejoiced to hear the rumor is unfounded. Her uncle's health is a matter of such supreme concern to Miss Julia's future—of course, when he dies, rumor has it, she inherits the whole fortune."

"Rumor seems to have been singularly active around here lately," I snapped.

"Can you blame it—when it is brought in in packages?" and before I could reply, the head waiter floated away to a distant table, approaching it with an air of solicitous concern.

I recalled Mr. Smats' instructions to the effect that we were not to remain away too long, and I tried to find Julia in the press of dancers, who seemed to be enjoying endless encores. She was nowhere in sight, apparently having entirely forgotten the impropriety of her dancing on the very evening of her uncle's death. On the other hand, had not this actually put the others, whoever they were, off the track, or at least puzzled them, to judge by the head waiter's questions?

I tried to eat some of the little globules of gelatine flavored with stale fish that passsed for caviare in this place, and gave it up. The cider mixed with bicarbonate of soda and labelled "champagne" was equally unattractive. I wondered if the contents of the flask, which still lay in my lap, were safe to drink.

The head waiter unexpectedly returned.

"Your check, sir," he said and offered me a paper folded on a plate.

I thought it might be a communication of some kind. I opened it and read "One hundred and twenty-five dollars for two suppers with cover charge."

"And how much am I expected to tip you?" I asked with what I hoped was becoming sarcasm.

"The minimum is of course ten per cent, but you will observe there was no charge for the flask."

"Are you in a hurry to have us go?"

"Oh, no, sir, but I thought you would want your check soon because Miss Julia would be wishing to return to her uncle—under the circumstances."

"Very thoughtful of you," I said fishing out my wallet. "If I should decline to pay this preposterous bill?" I asked.

"There is a policeman at the front door, sir," said the head waiter. "You wouldn't want a scandal that would involve Miss Julia, I feel sure. After one o'clock, we double our charges for all tables held beyond that hour."

I counted out one hundred and twenty-five dollars.

"And you can whistle for your tip," said I, piling the bills on the plate.

"I was afraid you would feel that way about it, sir," said the head waiter with an evil smile. "I expect I shall collect that another time, sir—when you will have cause to change your mind," and he picked up the plate of money and walked off. The last remark struck me as distinctly threatening.

In a few minutes Julia and Billy returned. The latter was very warm and he was struggling with a wilted collar that appeared to be strangling him. Julia appeared radiant, as if all recollection of the evening earlier had gone.

"What do you say we go on to Cerri Benito's—there's more room there," said Billy, taking a long drink out of the first glass his hand reached.

I resisted the temptation to retort that I was about to go on to my probable doom. Julia saved the situation.

"I think Cousin Robert and I ought to be going home. Uncle Howard wasn't feeling very well when we left and I don't want to risk disturbing him by coming in too late."

Once more I admired the fluency with which Julia could do it and I was thankful we were both in agreement not to publish Uncle Howard's death yet. As a matter of fact it was two minutes to one.

"By the way, William," I said, getting to my feet.

"Billy is what I'm called," he cut in, "my real name is Sebastian."

"Do you happen by any chance to know the name of the headwaiter here?"

"Sergius Sagerloop, the Swedish prince, is what they call him over the radio, but he used to be known over on Second Avenue as Michael Wort, from Oklahoma City.—He's billed to radio fans as the wistful warbler, and he's kind of a hard-boiled guy when you get down to brass tacks or knuckles. I saw him knock the Brooklyn Battler for a loop one night in a mix-up over a check. I heard afterwards though it was brass knuckles, so the K. O. wasn't made official."

This Mr. Billy, for I had not yet heard his family name, said to me as we made for the door.

"I hear he gave you personal attention tonight," Billy went on, as he searched through his overcoat pockets for his gloves. "He doesn't do that to many people for less than a hundred bone tip. The reporters will probably come around to ask you about it tomorrow. I gave him fifty dollars once the night after a Harvard game—just hoping for a little smile, and he put it in his pocket without even seeing me—what they call in psychology an automatic reflex. Gee, you're in luck."

"Isn't Billy wonderful?" said Julia. "He knows everything."

My own opinion of Billy I reserved for the present.

"Got room for me?—yes," said Billy, as he opened the door of the Packard before Evans could reach the handle. He followed Julia in, seating himself in the middle of the back seat, wrapping up one of Julia's hands between his as he did so.

"Lotsa room," he called encouragingly to me, when I hesitated for a second before entering my own car.

I began to wonder if a person with Billy's nerve might not be of use in the present emergency.

"Just drop me off wherever you like," said Billy. "I don't have to be anywhere in particular and I'm not going any place special— just on my way."

"Will you do me a favor, Billy?" I asked, making a sudden decision.

"Sure—but I've only got about ten dollars left," replied Billy, and began fumbling in his dinner jacket.

"It's not that," I said hastily. "Will you take Julia out to luncheon tomorrow—as my guests, both of you—and call for her at her uncle's house not later than twelve-thirty?"

"Every day on the same terms," Billy grinned.

It had crossed my mind that it might be important to get Julia out of the house and in broad daylight I did not see how the gang could prevent it.

"We'll expect you at twelve-thirty then."

"On the dot," replied Billy.

As we turned into the park to cross from the West to the East side, Billy sprang up, with the result that he smashed his hat flat against the top of the Packard.

"Just a moment," he called out.

I gave Martin the signal to stop, which we did so suddenly, that I saw the face of a traffic policeman peering in the window.

"Say!" said this apparition, "what's the big idea? Can't you signal your stop?"

"Not I," was my reply in a conciliatory tone, "you might take the question up with our Mr. Martin, the chauffeur, on the front seat."

"You're one of these wise-crackin' guys, ain't you?" the face at the window sputtered at me. "Just for that, let's see your license."

Martin handed me the precious document through the window and I held it out to the Celtic obstruction.

"I've a good mind to give you a ticket anyway," he growled, as he passed the paper back, and leaned against the door of the car, gazing meditatively down Central Park West.

Billy gave an indication that he desired to alight, but the broad back of the traffic officer blocked the door. In fact, Billy said: "You'll excuse me won't you, sir?" (This to me.) "I'm staying with Stuts Nash over on the West Side. So long, Julia, see you in the morning," and he laid his hand on the door.

"Drive on," said the traffic cop suddenly, and Martin took him at his word. Billy sprawled across our laps as a result of the unexpected jerk.

"I beg your pardon," he said, straightening out his hat for the second time.

Once more I pressed the buzzer and Martin brought the car to a halt, gently this time, just inside the park. Billy was half way out the door when the traffic policeman came up again, a whistle dangling nonchalantly from his lower lip.

"What are you guys playing—hop, skip, and jump or going to Jerusalem?" he asked, still, I thought, with unnecessary aggressiveness.

As for Billy, he still found it impossible to emerge because the policeman placed a firm hand on the door.

"Can't a gentleman alight from a car?" queried Billy with polite sarcasm, "or do you rate that as obstructing traffic?"

"Who asked you to butt in?" said the cop.

"I may have to butt out, if you keep on standing there," retorted Billy.

I began to grow extremely nervous. If Billy got into an altercation with the policeman we should all be arrested, and that would mean—what, I did not dare think.

"It's all right, officer," I called out cheerily. "We were just giving our friend a lift and stopped to let him off."

"I'm going to get out," Billy announced defiantly, and jammed his hat down over his ears, at the same time putting a shoulder well trained in football against the door. "Just a little practice in fundamentals—on the bucking-machine," he called out, and the door opened steadily with the policeman's feet sliding irresistibly across the pavement. Billy landed on the street beside the policeman, reached around him, and slammed the door of the car.

"Drive on," Billy called out, "I'll finish the argument."

"You're damned tooting, you will," said the policeman. "At the station house."

I called out to Martin, and over Julia's protest and, I think to Billy's surprise, we whizzed off into the darkness of the park.

"I hope he hasn't got the number of my car," I remarked gloomily, "but I suppose he has."

"I think it's a dirty trick to go off and leave Billy in trouble," said Julia.

"It's not over ten dollars' worth of trouble," I replied, "and a possible night in a cell, whereas if we go to the station house as witnesses, think what might—and would—happen."

"I think it's a shame," said Julia stubbornly. "Billy won't understand."

"He'll have to learn sooner or later to take some things on faith. This will be a good beginning for him."

# V
## THE BUTLER RETURNS—AND GOES

WHEN WE ARRIVED at the house in the East Eighties Mr. Smats' limousine was still before the door. Inside I saw two figures who, I assumed, were Mr. Smats' personal guardians. Across the street there was another dark and absolutely silent car. How many besiegers did it contain, I wondered? And when would they take action? And what action would they take? I confess I felt very uncomfortable as I opened the door of the house and followed Julia in. Why had I not had sense enough to send her away with Billy to some friends? I ought to get her out of the dangers of this house— but how? It was too late now; we were inside again. I cursed my stupidity for not having thought of using Billy earlier. Tomorrow might be too late. And Billy himself was probably under arrest by now for talking back to the policeman. Further, it was a hundred to one the officer had taken the number of our car and we should hear from him again. Why had Martin stopped our car so carelessly as to bring us under the eye of the traffic policeman? On such trifling events do the fates of empires sometimes turn.

Mr. Smats and Tommy welcomed us cheerfully. Uncle Howard was properly laid out in his own bed, Tommy said, and all arrangements had been completed for making it a death by natural causes. It suddenly occurred to me that Eloise had also been in the house all this time. How much had she seen or heard? How much did she know anyway?

"We're all set," Mr. Smats declared, interrupting my train of thought. "I suppose you sent the wire to the guy in Miami?"

"That I attended to when I called at my apartment for the package."

"One hundred and fifty thousand dollars," murmured Mr. Smats, sucking his tooth pick. "Real money? I wish I could believe it."

"Have the other servants come in?" I asked, for I knew that no argument of mine would be likely to allay Mr. Smats' justifiable suspicions.

"The whole procession from soup to nuts," replied Mr. Smats. "Tommy here broke the news to them one by one. He thought that better than letting the girl tell them. The girls all did the right thing, went off upstairs crying, and old frozen face—"

"Grierson, the butler?" I guessed at a venture.

"Yeah—well, he asked for one last look at his old master—alone. I didn't like that idea much myself," said Mr. Smats, noting my start, "so I gave him a spiel about doctor's orders and sent him upstairs with the others. I'll bet there's a hired help convention going on on the top floor right now."

"With Julia's maid, Eloise, talking the big headlines," added Tommy.

"I've asked you not to call me Julia," said that young lady.

"Sorry, but when you're all on a life raft together after the shipwreck, I just can't remember to be formal," Tommy replied.

"I think I should like to have a talk with Grierson—alone," I said.

Mr. Smats eyed me coolly, studied the tip of his ivory tooth pick and then reinserted that instrument in the corner of his mouth.

"Have it your own way," Mr. Smats answered, "only take my tip. He looks like a wise guy and may learn more than he will tell."

I went down to Uncle Howard's study where a summons on the bell produced Grierson after a slight interval.

"I beg pardon, sir," said that individual, "I understood, Mr. Cornua, that we had been dismissed for the night. I had to keep you waiting while I put on my coat and shoes again."

"Quite all right, Grierson," I replied. "Sit down, won't you? I want to ask you a few questions. You know, of course, that I was your master's best friend—that I am the executor of his estate, and all that?"

"Yes, sir."

I pushed a chair at Grierson and he reluctantly sat down. His face was the impassive mask of the well-trained butler. He did not differ in this respect from my man Evans, except that he was some ten or fifteen years older. His hair was thin on top and white at the temples. But his eyes, I noted, were keen and alert, watchful and more than a little suspicious. His hands were wiry and slender but his wrists showed that he was still, in spite of his age, a man of unusual muscular strength. That fact struck me as a little odd in a butler who had lived a sedentary life indoors for so many years.

"You were in the service here during Mrs. Birmingham's lifetime, I believe?" I asked casually, lighting a cigarette but watching Grierson's face, nevertheless.

"Yes, sir," he replied, "that would be—let me see—yes, two years after Miss Julia was born."

"Quite so," I went on. "Mr. Birmingham had just made his first great business success."

"I heard at the time, sir, that was why he bought this house and staffed it properly with servants."

"You had been a butler before?"

"I came with the best of references. Mr. Birmingham was not the man to put up with less, as you know."

"Yes. Then Mrs. Gorland died and Julia came to live here, because she, too, was all alone in the world."

"Yes, sir. May I enquire, sir, what is the purpose of all these questions? You'll pardon the liberty, I'm sure, if I point out that you know the answers as well as I do."

"I'm getting on to that, Grierson. Just be patient. I'm running things over in my mind to see if I've got them straight. You see, I shall have to manage Mr. Birmingham's fortune for Miss Julia, until she comes of age."

What I wished, for the moment, was to allay any doubts or suspicions in Grierson's mind. Also, I was wondering if I could find out about the photograph I had found in Howard Birmingham's watch.

"Did you know Miss Julia's mother?" I asked.

"I've seen her, once or twice, I believe—at dinners here."

I noted that he hesitated slightly and that his voice again took on the toneless quality of a perfect butler answering his master.

"What sort of a woman was she? She died the year I came back from Heidelberg—when Julia was a little baby?"

"I hardly know. Servants know very little, sir, about the guests in a house. We don't take the interest in such matters that we're supposed to. We have our own circles, you know, and trouble our heads very little about our betters."

"Was there any reason why you should gossip—about this lady?"

"About Mrs. Gorland? No, sir—at least, not to my knowledge. What's beneath the diamond necklace I have never made my business, sir."

"Rather handsome, wasn't she?"

"Some called her beautiful, but I daresay you've seen the photograph of her on Miss Julia's dresser."

"Yes, I have. Is that the only photograph of her in existence? That one shows her in her wedding gown. The veil rather obscures her hair and forehead."

"She was a beautiful woman," said Grierson thoughtfully. "Some say Miss Julia's the better-looking of the two. Not I. Miss Julia's pretty enough. I grant you—but she's modern, the slap dash kind. Her mother—but I beg your pardon, sir, you've set me chattering like an old maid with your questions out of the past."

During this speech in which Grierson seemed off his guard for a moment, like a man thinking aloud, I was wondering whether I dared lay my cards on the table and ask him about the photograph found in Howard Birmingham's watch. But perhaps he had been only evading my question about the existence of any more photographs.

"Is there another picture of Mrs. Gorland anywhere about, Grierson, besides the one on Miss Julia's dresser?"

"I don't think so—leastways, I've never seen one."

"Mrs. Gorland was Mrs. Birmingham's sister?"

"You're wrong, sir. She was her cousin—but they were like sisters, once upon a time—and then, they didn't see much of each other."

"Do you mean to say Mr. Birmingham was not Julia's uncle?"

I certainly started at this. All my life I had heard Julia refer to Mr. Birmingham as her "Uncle Howard."

"Only in a manner of speaking, sir. Miss Julia was brought up to think so, and that was what everyone was told. Even you, sir."

"But why?"

"I don't know, sir, and I've only told you this much because the truth would come out in proving Mr. Birmingham's will."

"Grierson," I said suddenly, making up my mind at last, "have you ever seen this?" and I thrust under his nose the little photograph I had taken from Howard's watch.

The change in the man was startling. He rose from his chair with a choking, gurgling noise in his throat, and stretched out a grey, shaking hand that seemed to turn into a claw with the effort it made to snatch the picture from my hand.

"You've no right to that!" he croaked hoarsely.

Then as by a great effort he pulled himself together and sank back in his chair.

"I beg your pardon, sir," he said, mopping his forehead with a colored silk handkerchief, the edges of which were somewhat frayed, and sinking back in his chair. "It fair upset me for a moment to see the picture from Mr. Birmingham's watch in your hands. Then I recollected, sir, you are his executor and entitled to examine all his belongings."

"So you knew the picture as one he carried in his watch?"

"Bless you, sir, you can't be butler in a house for eighteen years without picking up and putting back in their places things belonging to the family. I've found Mr. Birmingham's watch on his desk a dozen times with the case open."

"Why were you so moved when you saw this picture in my hands?"

"Good Lord, sir, you catch a person up so. Just for a moment I forgot it was your right to touch such things. You see, Mr. Birmingham meant a lot to me, even if I was only a butler."

"Have you any idea why Mr. Birmingham carried a picture of Mrs. Gorland in his watch case instead of a picture of his wife?"

"No more idea than you as a man of the world, sir, has already guessed."

"Did you ever know Mr. Gorland?"

"No, sir." For an appreciable moment he paused before resuming. "They did say, sir, that he was killed out in South Africa. I never heard the details. It all happened before I came into Mr. Birmingham's service."

"And how old was Miss Julia when you entered Mr. Birmingham's service?"

"How old?"

"That was my question, Grierson."

"Miss Julia was two years old when I came here to Mr. Birmingham."

I saw him again mop his face, as he made this answer, and on his forehead beads of sweat kept forming.

"How long before you came here did Mr. Gorland die?"

"I don't rightly know, sir. I don't know at all!"

"Why should this question so move you? Surely, if, as you say, you take no interest in your betters, the death of a man you never heard of until afterwards was no concern of yours?"

"I spoke stronger than I meant, sir. My master's sudden taking off—I served his luncheon to him only a few hours ago—has fair upset me. I don't know what I am saying."

"You have no idea of the exact date of Mr. Gorland's death?"

"No, sir."

"Approximately, how long ago was it, before you came?"

"Can't say, sir."

"Are you sure?"

"Absolutely. I was a complete stranger to all the family."

"Miss Julia was two years old?"

"Yes, sir."

"Then Mr. Gorland's death must have occurred at furthest back, about not quite three years before you came?"

"I don't know, sir."

"What did he die of?"

"I never heard, sir."

"Is he dead?" I asked, with a sudden intuition. I call it that because I don't know how these ideas come to us.

Grierson leaned forward and stared at me with a long, searching look. I saw the careful veneer of the butler's stoic expression fade from his face to be replaced with the look of a man whom I should not care to meet in physical combat. Whatever other inference one might draw, it was clear, I decided, that Grierson had not always been a butler. But I was equally surprised to see him suddenly resume the butler's face, modified only by a slightly contemptuous smile.

"I see," he said, "I suppose all of the servants are under suspicion, in a manner of speaking, sir. You're having a shot yourself at playing detective, Mr. Cornua. But if you think there's anything suspicious about Mr. Birmingham's taking off, why don't you call in the police?"

"Why should you assume that I suspect the servants of anything? You've heard the doctor say the death was from natural causes."

"Yes, so I've heard. But I know something this odd looking doctor upstairs doesn't know. Mr. Birmingham's own physician gave him a complete physical examination yesterday—Mr. Birmingham himself told me afterwards when I had showed the doctor out—and he certified Mr. Birmingham as in excellent condition for a man of his age. Blood-pressure satisfactory—heart normal—kidneys O. K., sir. Just a bit strange he should drop dead the next day and his own physician not be called in."

"I tried to get Dr. Spargill on the 'phone, of course, but he had left for Miami to take over an emergency case down there."

"How about Dr. Spurlee who handles the practice when Dr. Spargill is away, and knows Mr. Birmingham almost as well?"

"I didn't know about him. I naturally turned to the first doctor I did know."

"Do you want to know what I think, Mr. Cornua?"

"Well?"

"I think it's a case of murder. Put that in your pipe and smoke it, sir, meaning no offence. Murder."

"Murder?" I said, trying to feign surprise.

"You've known it right along, if you'll pardon the liberty. I saw it in your face when I first came back. Murder—and you know it is murder, Mr. Cornua. Now, I ask you a question, sir—as man to man. Why haven't you called in the police?"

"There is at present a very good reason, Grierson. There is for example the scandal—and the shock this knowledge would cause Miss Julia."

Of course I did not dare be frank with this man, for I remembered the questions he had not answered—the one about whether Mr. Gorland was dead, for instance, and the unpleasant looks I had seen on Grierson's face.

"Very well, sir. You're the best judge of your own business. But I have my responsibility, too, to consider, sir. Unless you give me a better reason, I am going down to the telephone in the servants' hall and call headquarters."

Again he leaned forward and studied my face with an unpleasant insolence. I resented being classed among the suspects by a man whose own attitude was highly suspicious.

"Just let me run over a few points in this business as they would strike an outsider, Mr. Cornua. Mr. Birmingham is found lying dead. Instead of calling in either his regular doctor's assistant, if, as you say, the regular doctor is away, you bring into this house a young doctor who is a total stranger and a man who is pretty well-known in certain parts of this city. I refer to Mr. Smats."

"How do you happen to know Mr. Smats?"

"You'll have to think that over for yourself. Just let me finish. You and Miss Julia go out on a strange errand—returning about an hour after midnight."

"One twenty-nine, to be precise," I said.

"All right, sir. You leave this stranger doctor and your other friend in charge of the body and of the house. We, the servants, are hustled down into the servants' hall and told to stay there. As a special concession, I'm allowed a look from the door into Mr. Birmingham's rooms, where I see him laid out in the bed under the careful guard of your friends. You send for me down here and ask a lot of questions which prove you've got more than a suspicion of murder in your mind—and yet you won't send for the police. Then you pull out a picture which belongs in Mr. Birmingham's watch—which you had no right to touch until there has been an investigation. I said you had a right a moment ago, to lead you on, sir. But you know you haven't. What's it all about, sir? That's what I ask you. Where do you come in to this?"

"I come in to this as the only responsible friend Miss Julia has in the world."

"Then you'd better send for the police, sir, and have this matter cleared up. And if you won't, I will. That's flat!"

"Grierson," I said, panic stricken at the possible consequences his action would involve us all in, "will you trust me for the present? Will you believe me when I say I have good reasons for my actions, and that just now it is not possible to have the police here?"

"You're a gentleman, Mr. Cornua—and you try to take advantage of being a gentleman. Well, sir, to be franker with you than you have been with me, I have been a gentleman in my time. I may have been a butler for a good many years until the butler-lingo has become almost second nature to me, but I was a gentleman. That's why you and I must do business as equals or not at all. I'll give you five minutes exactly to convince me not to call the police," and with these words Grierson took out a large loud-ticking butler's silver watch.

I hesitated unable to make up my mind whether I was being bluffed by an astute man or whether I should run all the risks of frankness and assume that Grierson could be turned into an ally.

"Four minutes left," I heard him say.

With a sudden desperate resolve, I took the plunge and narrated to Grierson all the details as I have set them down in these pages. When I finished he snapped shut with a click the case of his watch, crammed it into his waistcoat pocket, and stared at me.

"If I'm not mistaken," he said slowly, "you've made a rare mess of this case. We'll have to leave the police out of the murder side of this"—I breathed with relief at these words—"and go at this thing from the Garden of Aphrodite angle. But I think, Mr. Cornua, that your actions have made the cornering of the criminals impossible. However, we'll have a try with one of them—that girl Eloise up-stairs—Miss Julia's maid."

"Her maid? But—but—"

"It was she who told me Mr. Birmingham's body was found in Miss Julia's dressing room. You've told me she had no chance to get in there. Well, then, how did she know?"

"You said something about having been a gentleman once. What do you mean? Who are you, Grierson?"

"If I was to tell you that story—now, Mr. Cornua, we shouldn't finish before daylight. I'll bring Eloise down," and he closed the door softly after him as he left the room. I took out the picture I had found in Howard Birmingham's watch, and was, therefore, startled, because lost in thought, when Grierson suddenly opened the door again.

"By the way," he remarked, watching me hastily put away the picture, "better make certain Miss Julia doesn't interrupt us. We may have to use a little third-degree stuff on Eloise," and he closed the door again.

I had an uncomfortable feeling that he had reopened the door with the deliberate intention of taking me by surprise. I stepped up to Julia's room, however, and tapped on the door. She opened it and I caught a glimpse of her in a shimmery pink silk dressing gown trimmed with white fur. She looked adorable.

"Julia, dear," I said, "don't come down to the study for the present. I am going to question some more of the servants and it is better not to interrupt."

"You silly goose, Bobbie, I hadn't the slightest intention of butt-ing in. Go and play Sherlock Holmes all by yourself. I certainly don't want to play Dr. Watson. Kiss me good night, Bobbie."

This was an invitation not to be refused, for Julia kissed me only on special occasions, such as birthdays and Christmas or when I brought her little presents. She had the good sense to make her kisses a matter of importance.

When I returned to the study I found Grierson standing beside an angry and sulky young woman who had on over her nightgown a rather short flannel jacket which she held together at her throat with one hand. Her bare feet were thrust into a discarded pair of Julia's slippers.

"I don't know by what right," Eloise spluttered, "that you drag me down here in my night clothes—"

"I told you Mr. Cornua would make it worth your while, Eloise," said Grierson suavely, "and as for your night clothes, you don't often find them embarrassing."

"Shut your dirty face," retorted the young woman.

"Perhaps, if you retired for a moment and slipped on something more suitable," I murmured, blushing slightly. I did not, of course, know what Grierson's experience had been, but as for me, I was at that time a bachelor.

"Not she," said Grierson, "and rouse the other servants. You'll stay here as you are. It's not cold and the heat is on."

"What do I get out of this. Speak quick," she said, "or I'll let out a scream that will shake the plaster off the ceiling."

"No, you will not scream," said Grierson, and he stepped up close to her and laid his hand eloquently on her throat: "Just a little pressure of thumb and forefinger," he went on pleasantly, "and the scream doesn't even get going."

"I'm scared," she said. "What have I done? What you got on me, Jerry?"

"Now, take it easy, Mary—"

"Eloise," I interrupted.

"Oh, that's only her professional name. This is Mary Dooggin, otherwise known as the lady's maid Eloise Carnet."

"What do I get?" reiterated Mary, as I must now call her.

"It all depends on what you've got to sell, Mary dear," said Grierson. "The law of supply and demand, of which you may have heard. But for your temporarily hurt feelings and informal dress, say a retainer of twenty-five dollars, which Mr. Cornua will now place in your right hand."

I took the hint and counted out the bills over which her hand clenched determinedly. The money seemed to give Mary confidence, for she smiled and relaxed her hold on her dressing gown.

The result was the exposure of considerably more throat than Grierson needed to use in stopping a scream.

"Sit here, Mary," said Grierson, "and I'll just stand conveniently close behind you. Now tell Mr. Cornua what you know about this business upstairs."

I noted that Grierson leaned over the back of the arm chair his hands resting near her throat in case the threat of the scream should be again attempted.

"I don't know anything about it," she said stubbornly.

Grierson bent over her from above and spoke harshly into her face.

"Mary, if you come across, it means easy money for you—but if you don't, I'll tell some things I know about you—and they're not Sunday school stories either."

I disliked intensely Grierson's method of approach, but somehow I did not seem to be able to do anything about it.

"Jerry, you can't bluff me that way. I'm not a lady with a reputation to save—I admit I've been on parties—who cares about a lady's maid? I've got my own life to live—as I damn please."

"I did not labor under the delusion that I could frighten you about your moral reputation, Mary—but possibly Miss Julia's string of pearls would be a more effective argument."

Mary jumped as if stung and whirled about in her chair to face Grierson's sneering smile.

"What do you mean?"

"I know where they are—in your trunk. I found them there the other day—and kept the information to myself until it should come in handy."

"I—I thought they were imitation," sobbed Mary.

"Banana oil," remarked Grierson dispassionately. "I credit you with too much intelligence to steal phony stuff."

"What bearing on our particular question has all this?" I intervened. "Surely, we can take up the matter of Miss Julia's pearls in the morning."

"Everything is relevant in a horse-trade," replied Grierson. "Mary, what do you know?"

"Jerry, I swear to God I'm not in on the murder-stuff."

"How do you know there has been a murder?" Grierson cut in sharply. "I haven't said so."

"Banana oil," retorted Mary with a smile and calmly scratched one of her bare knees. "You didn't haul me out of bed in my nightgown to look at my figure. It's easier to go to The Follies. So we can all play the same game, Jerry—Miss Julia's pearls against your murder. I guess the murder has the biggest cash possibilities. Now I'll tell you men one thing—and get this straight, both of you. You can't hang this murder on me just because there's a string of pearls in my trunk. If you try—well, there'll be two more men sitting in that electric chair up the river. If it's to be a horse-trade, let's get our understanding complete."

"Would you mind stating your case more specifically?" I interjected. The situation was getting so complex my mind could not analyze it.

"All right. I'm not afraid of you—either of you, see? Jerry here can choke me, if he dares, but he won't because he's near enough sitting on a hot griddle as it is. As for you, Mr. Cornua, I've a hunch somebody is pulling your leg—but that's your party, not mine. If you want to see me do the hula-hula in my nightie because you think it would shock my sensitive nerves, you've got me wrong. When it comes to stacking up against a murder I can play Eve in her innocence and not bat an eye. Now before I tell my story, let's find out how much it will cost you for me to keep still about your little mix-up."

Just about this time I began seriously to question the policy of cross-examining the servants. It seemed to add to the cost and the complexity of the problem without in any way aiding in the solution. And yet in every detective-story I had ever read, the principle was laid down, at least by implication, that the investigator should "grill" (I believe that is the proper term) the servants.

"Mr. Cornua is prepared to pay adequately for all information that proves to be important," said Grierson with what I thought was an ill-timed attempt to resume the authoritative tone of a butler.

"Is he also prepared to pay what I want for not giving certain information to the police? When I went to school Jerry, they told me speech is silver but silence is golden."

"You think you can prove something against a man of Mr. Cornua's reputation and position? Don't be silly."

"All right. Let's have the police in and arbitrate this. You tell 'em, Jerry, about the pearls in my trunk, and I'll tell 'em to go upstairs and give Mr. Birmingham the once-over, and we'll see which interests 'em most. Perfectly fair, I call it."

"What would you consider a fair offer to keep silent until I release you? I appeal to your sense of justice, Miss Eloise—er—Mary. I want to find the murderer—but I feel that any premature publicity might—er—might not—er—be in—er—the best interests, so to speak, of all concerned."

I sensed that my appeal was heard as a lame argument.

"I like to do business with a business man and not with a hardboiled butler," said Mary. "This is no lump sum proposition, see? I sell on the installment plan—so much down and the rest in monthly payments."

"You see," said Grierson, "you can't prove anything because there is nothing to prove. You would be one of the suspects yourself if you called in the police."

"Yes, and I'd give a nickel, Jerry, to know why *you* don't want 'em called in. Now, I'll tell you something more. I've got an alibi for this afternoon that nothing can upset—see? Supposing I should admit the pearl job, which I don't, because you planted the pearls on me, Jerry. But they don't fry you for taking pearls. So if you don't want the police in here, why not pay what your wish is worth? And Jerry, darling—I've just thought of something else. If I do call the police in, and you hang the pearls on me, I'll put up my defence that it's a frame-up to get a poor, innocent girl in trouble and throw suspicion on me—and it will look like that when they find out about the other thing. Boy, I'm sitting on the top of the world!"

"All right," said Grierson suddenly. "Call in the police. And we'll see what that will get you."

"No—no!" I cried. "Not that—er—I mean—not until this mystery has been cleared up—"

I saw Mary turn and look me over very carefully and shrug her shoulders off which both dressing gown and night dress had rather carelessly slipped.

"What are you getting paid, Jerry?" she asked.

"Not a cent. I am assisting Mr. Cornua in a cause of justice."

"Banana oil," replied Mary, "and a fat chance I'd have had against the pair of you if I hadn't been able to hold you up in turn. Jerry had an idea he could put me through the third degree, I guess—twist my wrists and make me confess—that was going to be your game, Jerry, wasn't it? That's why you wanted me practically naked so you could hurt me easier. Well, boys, you've got another guess coming. Little Mary learned how to take care of herself the year following the big wind. When you work for nothing, Jerry, it's because your own skin is in danger. Mr. Cornua doesn't want the police—and you don't, Jerry, and I'll leave this thought with Mr. Cornua: the reasons are different. But what do I care? I've got to have my money."

It did occur to me that Grierson—Jerry, as Mary called him— had accepted without much question my argument for not calling in the police, but I had laid it at the time to his loyalty and affection for Mr. Birmingham and Miss Julia in whose house he had been a butler for so many years. But now Mary had aroused my suspicions against him once more. Why had he dragged her into this—and why had he brutally brought her downstairs in her nightgown, a really indefensible act from the point of view of any proper motive, unless he wished to discredit Mary in my eyes by making me believe she was a wantonly immoral woman? Indeed, that had been his first line of attack upon her in his question. Reckless and immoral she might be, and yet her courage, even though it were the blackmailer's courage, did not seem to me to be the reflection of a mind guilty of murder.

Grierson! Who was he before he became a butler? A gentleman, he said, using the word in its cant servants' hall meaning— that is, a person able to employ butlers. And I recalled that he had evaded my questions about Mr. Gorland. Had he any mysterious connection with the clouded past of Julia's mother and Howard Birmingham? Was he perhaps an instrument of vengeance?

"Well?" Mary's voice spoke sharply.

"Quite so, Mary," I replied. "Suppose you see me privately in the morning when we can come to some mutually satisfactory understanding."

"Suits me," she answered, "but if you leave the house without seeing me first, I call up the police."

"Shall we leave it at that?" I suggested.

She stood up and drew the dressing jacket up over her bare shoulders and turned to Grierson.

"The next time you set a trap, Jerry," she grinned, snapping her fingers under his nose, "don't leave your own foot behind for bait."

With this she opened the door and with a swish of her thin nightgown, closed the door after her. Grierson coughed a slight butler's cough, seated himself in the armchair Mary had just left, and chose one of Howard's cigars. He snipped off the end with a gold cutter on the other end of his watch chain, produced a gold cigarette lighter from his waistcoat pocket and lit the corona corona.

"Shall we open a bottle of the '79 port?" he asked, as he let the first whiff of his cigar trickle out through his nostrils.

"Not for me, thanks," I said. "It is three thirty-nine and eleven seconds. I never drink between two and ten a. m."

"We are back where we were, Mr. Cornua. How did Mary—or Eloise perhaps is the name to resume to avoid making Miss Julia curious if she hears you use the other—how did she know that—that—well, I shall remember the proprieties—how did she know that Mr. Birmingham's body was found in Miss Julia's dressing room—unless she was in the house when the murder was committed?"

"Possibly she listened at the door or looked through the keyhole while Tommy and Mr. Smats were arranging things."

"Oh, that was their job, eh? While you got Julia out of the house."

"Miss Julia—if you please."

"I'm not butler here any more, Cornua. Julia from now on."

I resented his tone and his further deliberate dropping of the mister from before my name.

"What I don't see, Cornua, is what you and your accomplices—I beg pardon, your friends—are going to do next—no, please don't interrupt. Your predicament interests me as an intellectual problem, and your colossal nerve magnificently masked as naive innocence commands my most profound admiration."

He blew several smoke-rings while staring upward at the elaborate plaster ornaments on Howard's study-ceiling.

"I do not see what is to be gained by your forgetting your place and becoming insulting," I retorted.

"No—perhaps you are right. I suppose it has occurred to you that a prominent businessman and multi-millionaire like Mr. Birmingham cannot die even of natural causes without headlines across all the New York papers—and that however speedy you may be in hurrying your late friend underground there will arrive upon our doorstep a host of exceedingly shrewd young reporters with several hundred clever and embarrassing questions? I hope you have a sufficient supply of answers."

"I know the heavy consequences of my policy," I said stiffly.

"Policy?" he murmured to himself. "Well, Mr. Cornua, I am taking a train that leaves the Grand Central at four-thirty a. m. I see I have ample time, but I shall face the journey with more peace of mind if I have an extra supply of ready money. May I ask you how much cash you have on your person? I realize that this has been an expensive evening for you and possibly the roll may be wearing thin."

"You are not going to leave this house," I said, springing to my feet.

"No—and who is to stop me? Not you, Cornua—it wouldn't do. The telephone has not been disconnected."

"Suppose I am the one who sends for the police?"

"I've considered that and rejected the hypothesis as too improbable. Besides, I have a clear conscience and am perfectly ready to talk things over with them. But if you choose not to send for them,

I really don't see that I can be of any further service in a business that does not concern me personally. I am going."

The arm of the law is long, I reflected, and it would not be likely that Mr. Jerry Grierson could get far enough away to be out of reach. For the moment it would simplify my position to let him go. He was watching my face and I saw him smile suddenly when I had reached this mental conclusion.

"You have a most expressive countenance, Cornua. He who runs may read it. I am glad you have resolved to be reasonable."

I took out my pocket book and looked over the contents. Five hundred and sixteen dollars was all the cash I had on hand. I am not one of those ostentatious persons who carry a lot of money about with them. I was annoyed to discover Grierson peering over my shoulder as I ran through my wallet. He stretched out his hand.

"It will have to do for the present," he said. "I'll telegraph for more funds when I need them—but this will buy me a railway ticket and a modest lower-berth. Give my love to Eloise, won't you?" and before I could say more, he slipped through the door.

Five moments later I heard the front door close softly. I happened to be looking at my watch at the moment, checking up on the time left before Grierson's train was due to leave, and I noted that it was exactly eleven seconds after he closed the door that I heard three pistol shots in rapid succession in the street outside.

# VI
## THE POLICE RUSH IN

I STARTED TOWARD THE WINDOW to draw back the curtains and peer out—for a horrible misgiving seized me—when I heard the shrill blast of a police whistle, followed by the pounding of a night-stick on the flagstones. I knew that this was a policeman's signal for help. Also I heard the noise of a motor starting off west, and the shouts evidently of a policeman. Before I could reach the window there was a violent ringing of the front door bell and a pounding on the panels of the door.

As I hurried into the hall, I saw Julia's frightened face at the top of the stairs and close behind her the equally disturbed faces of Mr. Smats and Tommy.

"Go back," I shouted. "I am going to open the front door."

Indeed, I began to wonder if the panels would last until I could reach it. Police whistles seemed to be shrilling from every point of the compass. Julia slipped into her room again and Mr. Smats and Tommy vanished. I flung back the front door and two patrolmen entered carrying a body.

"This guy just left this house and a bunch in a taxi across the street shot him down."

"Grierson!" I exclaimed.

"Well, that's part of what we want to know," said the leading policeman. "Got a couch handy? I guess he's done for."

I led the way once more into Howard's study. The police followed and laid Grierson down on the sofa. The first policeman took off his cap and wiped his forehead with a handkerchief. Several

66

more policemen began to crowd through the still open front door and into the room.

"Lucky I turned the corner just as I did," said the first policeman, addressing the others. "I got the number of the taxi that bumped this guy off," and he turned to the telephone.

I listened to him giving details to headquarters, including the number of the taxi.

"Yeah, and there was a Lincoln limousine out in front that beat it off, too. . . . No, didn't get that number. But there's a Packard still there with a chauffeur and we're holding that."

Evans, in my car, I thought. Good Lord, what a complicated mess.

"Whose house is this?" he said turning to me.

"Mr. Howard Birmingham's," I replied.

"Sure, I know that. What I mean is, where is he? Bring him down, mister, will you?"

"I can't," I said, "he died suddenly of heart failure this evening."

"Gentleman here says Mr. Birmingham croaked this evening," said the policeman into the telephone receiver. "Sure—just a minute. What's your name?" and he turned to me.

"Robert Cornua—a friend of the family."

"Address?"

"6937 Park Avenue."

"Business?"

"Student of philosophy."

"Student—at your age, mister?"

"Yes."

"S'funny." And he repeated the information into the telephone. "All right, chief. We'll hold everything," and he hung up.

An ambulance clanged up at the door, followed by a patrol wagon. A brisk young man in a white jacket entered followed by more police and a police sergeant.

The brisk young man went over to Grierson's body on the sofa and made a business like and rapid inspection. He wrote his findings down on a pad.

"They sure got him," he remarked, wetting the end of his pencil, "three times. One would have been enough. Looks like a Colt automatic job—the autopsy ought to show. Guess I better wait and give the detective my evidence."

"Sure, doc," said the first policeman. "Chief Detective Killark and some of the Homicide Squad will be here in a few minutes. We'll wait for orders. Do you know this man, Mr. Cornua?"

"Yes. He was Mr. Birmingham's butler. Jerry Grierson—the name."

The officer wrote my reply in his notebook and then strolled about the room, glancing casually at this and that. Meanwhile I was a prey to many disturbing emotions. What would be the outcome? I wanted very much to consult Mr. Smats upstairs and to get some reassuring word to Julia, but it seemed hopeless. The bulk of two large policemen completely occupied the door into the hallway. The other policemen stood nonchalantly about, waiting. Now and then two or three of them spoke together in low tones and there would be a laugh, as if they were exchanging funny stories. I sat in the armchair and tried to think the situation out, but the atmosphere of the room was not conducive to analytical thought. And then Detective Killark and some more men—members of the Homicide Squad—arrived preceded by the shrieking siren of their car.

Detective Killark wore a grey felt hat on the back of his head and gave immediate evidence of possessing a brusque manner.

"Which officer saw the shooting?" he asked, after a brief and uninterested glance at Grierson.

"I did, sir," said the first policeman stepping forward.

"Let's see your shield. You're the patrolman on this beat?"

"Yes, sir."

"Why didn't you get the number of the limousine that drove off?"

"I rushed over to the man who was shot. Thought I might get a word from him if he hadn't been instantly killed."

"A mistake. You ought to have got the car. Did you fire on the taxi?"

"No, sir."

"Why not?"

"When I looked up from the man who was shot, it was gone."

"Next time I advise you to use your head."

"Yes, sir."

"Now, we'll hear you, if you please."

This was spoken to me. I repeated all the information, including that about my name, address and occupation, which I had already given to the patrolman.

"Did you see this man Grierson—the butler, you called him—leave the house?"

"No."

"Did you see him before he went?"

"Yes."

"Where?"

"In this room."

"Why? What was he doing in here?"

"He came in to tell me he was leaving."

"Where—did he tell you that?"

"To the Grand Central—to take a train at four thirty."

"Did he give you any explanation?"

"No."

"Did you ask him for one?"

"No."

"Didn't it seem to you queer for the butler to be leaving in the middle of the night?"

"I didn't think about it."

The detective paused and looked at me. I sensed that for some reason he did not like this reply.

"What were you doing sitting up all night?"

"I am the executor of Mr. Birmingham's will as well as a friend of the family and I was thinking over the responsibilities that had come to me."

"Is that your Packard and chauffeur outside?"

"Yes."

"Who are the two men in it?"

"My chauffeur and my valet."

"Mr. Birmingham has a niece?"

"Yes."

"Where is she?"

"Upstairs."

"How about the other servants?"

"They are upstairs, too."

"Has Mr. Birmingham spoken to you lately about any threatening letters?"

"No."

"Have you any reason to believe that anyone would have a reason for killing him?"

"Mr. Birmingham?"

"You heard me?"

"Certainly not."

"You mean 'no'?"

"Yes."

"Then you don't think that gang in the taxi was waiting for Mr. Birmingham and shot the butler by mistake?"

I was immensely relieved when this question revealed the drift of Detective Killark's questioning.

"I have no reason to think so. As far as I know Mr. Birmingham hasn't an enemy in the world. At least—he never gave me any indication of such a thing—and I have talked his affairs over intimately with him for years."

"You're no theory about this shooting?"

"None. It's a mystery to me."

"That will do for the present, Mr. Cornua. Send up for Miss Gorland."

"But surely—at this time of night?"

"Sorry, Mr. Cornua—but this is a murder case. We can't observe the social conventions of your set just now."

In a moment or two Julia entered the room in her pink satin dressing gown trimmed with white fur. She stared wide-eyed and frightened at me and I gave her what I hoped she would infer was a reassuring smile. I had never seen her look more beautiful. Even the detective was impressed by her beauty, for he laid the stub of his cigar down on the edge of the table.

"You are Miss Julia Gorland?"

"Yes."

I was glad to hear the firmness with which she spoke the monosyllable.

"Sorry, miss, to get you up at this hour, but can you identify this body here?"

I saw Julia start and give another hurried look at me. Then she walked over to the couch.

"It's Grierson—the butler! What's happened?" she exclaimed. "Is he dead?"

"Yes. Now Miss Gorland—be calm, if you please, and pay great attention to my questions. When did you last see this man alive?"

"When he served luncheon to uncle and me this afternoon."

"You haven't seen him this evening?"

"No."

"Did you ever hear your uncle say anything about him?"

"Only that he was a good butler."

"Do you know if your uncle had any enemies? Have you any reason to suppose he had?"

Julia glanced again at me, but I was careful to give no sign for I saw the detective watching us keenly.

"No," she said, but I knew the detective had noted the slight pause.

"Was he a good uncle to you?"

"Oh, yes."

"How long ago did your mother die?"

"When I was three months old."

"That was about twenty years ago?"

"Nineteen," said Julia demurely.

"And your father?"

"He—went away—to South Africa. I have never heard from him since."

"You are an orphan then?"

"Yes."

"And Mr. Birmingham has looked after you ever since?"

"Like a father."

I started at these words because it flashed across my mind that Howard Birmingham might have been this child's father. I could not get that photograph in the watchcase out of my head.

"He's left you well provided for, I suppose?"

"He has left me everything, so Cousin Bobbie says."

"Cousin Bobbie?"

"Mr. Cornua here."

"Oh, I see. That's Cousin Bobbie is it? Well, well."

Chief Detective Killark walked up and down the room for a minute and a half, deep in thought.

"That will be all for the present, Miss Gorland. Go to your room and try to get some sleep. We may have to ask you a lot of tiring questions tomorrow."

Julia turned to me, but I nodded and smiled: "Good night, little girl," I said. She left with a puzzled look on her face.

"It's a very large estate, Mr. Cornua?" the detective asked after Julia had gone.

"Probably about thirty millions net, as near as I can judge."

"You are a man of independent means yourself?"

"I inherited about seven millions from my father and I have never speculated. The income was more than I required, so the principal has increased."

"Mr. Birmingham has no other relatives besides his niece?"

"None."

"You can furnish me proof tomorrow about the value of your own estate and its present financial condition?"

"Yes—but I don't see—"

"The fees of the trustee of an estate like Mr. Birmingham's are large, Mr. Cornua. I want to be sure you don't need the money."

"God bless my soul."

Mr. Killark ignored my ejaculation of surprise.

"This is a queer case, Mr. Cornua. This man Grierson was a mistake. Somebody is after bigger fish. Now you and Miss Gorland have been holding something back on me. That will be another mistake—and one that might have unpleasantness for the young lady. So you change your advice to her tomorrow. You've got to be frank with me, Mr. Cornua, unless you want me to go at the whole thing from another angle."

"I don't believe I understand—"

"Sure you do. I saw the young lady trying to get her cue from you—not certain what or how much she ought to tell until you gave her a high sign. You couldn't tip her off, so she shut up like a clam and played safe with all my questions. Well, you think it over while I rout out some more of these servants."

Mr. Killark strolled to the door and looked out.

"What did you find on the butler, Bill," he said to one of his squad who had been examining Grierson's body.

"About four hundred dollars and some loose change, a gold cigarette lighter, gold cigar cutter, cheap silver watch, rolled gold chain, three keys and an address."

"What address?"

Bill, as he was called, held out a slip of paper.

"Funny," said Mr. Killark taking it. "Any particular reason Mr. Cornua, why Mr. Birmingham's butler should elope with your address?"

"He often came to my apartment with messages from Mr. Birmingham."

"Errand boy as well as butler, eh? He ought to have some more addresses on him in that case."

"Nothing else," said Bill.

"Half his jewelry phony—the watch and chain—and half of it solid gold—the lighter and cigar cutter. Either of them Mr. Birmingham's?" and Mr. Killark held them out for my inspection.

"No, I don't recognize them."

"Wonder why he had to have a note of your address if he came there often? Short memory is a bad thing, Mr. Cornua."

"I can't say," I replied.

"Well, maybe you will later. By the way, Mr. Cornua, you don't suppose that butler knew too much, do you?"

"What do you mean?"

"Well, I just threw it out as a suggestion. I think I'll call in another witness. I suppose Miss Gorland would have a personal maid?"

"Yes, Mary—I mean Eloise Carnet."

"Why did you call her Mary?"

"I got her confused with another one."

"Oh, then Miss Gorland hasn't had this one long?"

"I don't know."

"Mike, just go upstairs and sing out on the top floor for Eloise, will you? Pound on the doors until you wake her up, if necessary. You stay here, Mr. Cornua. I may want the benefit of your—advice—when I see this woman. Make it snappy, Mike."

Five minutes elapsed before Mike was heard returning accompanied by the protesting voice of Mary. During this time Mr. Killark sat at the table and chewed a cigar, while he kept picking up first one and then the other of the objects found on Grierson.

"The cigarette lighter is a brand new model—hasn't had it long—but the cigar cutter is an old timer—worn pretty smooth and the design old-fashioned. Humph."

Mr. Killark appeared to be thinking aloud.

"How about me and the ambulance?" queried the young man in the white jacket.

"Sure, run along. We'll take your evidence in the morning, and I'll send this to the morgue in the patrol wagon, if there's nothing else. So long, Doc. Much obliged."

"Don't mention it."

The young man left.

Mike ushered in Mary, who had paused to put on more attire than she wore when I saw her last.

"Glory to the saints—the cops!" she cried.

"That's a good French accent," remarked Mr. Killark. "Eloise, is your name Mary?"

"And what if it is? Sure Eloise is the name I use in my job. You've got to be toney to get away with my stuff."

"Mary what?"

"Dooggin."

"Alias Eloise Carnet?"

"No alias about it, and you can't prove anything on me. I told Mr. Cornua about Miss Julia's pearls being in my trunk for safe keeping—she going out and leaving them lying about—and the lord knows who tramping in and out of the house."

Mary was frightened, I could see that, and fear loosened her tongue so that she reverted to type.

"Did you know the pearls were in Mary's trunk, Mr. Cornua?"

"Sure he does," Mary cut in. "Wasn't I after telling him and Jerry Grierson about them in this very room—my God, what's that?" and she let out a piercing scream when she suddenly caught sight of Grierson's body on the sofa.

"Jerry Grierson, the butler, was shot and killed, Mary, as he left this house—by some gunmen in a taxicab. Now pull yourself together, my girl, because I've got some questions for you."

"You'd better ask him first," said Mary screaming at the top of her voice and pointing at me.

"I'll ask him when I get good and ready. You come first. Now, what were you doing in this room with the butler and Mr. Cornua when you were talking about pearls?"

"They tried to hang the pearls on me—the dirty double cross-ers—and I gave 'em as good as they got. To keep me mouth shut, I says, will cost you a pretty penny, I says—I'm no cheap piker—I'm installment plan goods—so much down, I says, and so much a month—for, life, I says."

"Possibly I could explain," I intervened because it was quite clear that Mary's story would be misinterpreted by Mr. Killark.

"Possibly you could," he retorted, "but you won't just yet. What were you to keep your mouth shut about, Mary?"

"About the funny business upstairs, to be sure, after Mr. Birmingham's body was found."

"What's that," cried Killark, starting toward her with an entire change of tone. "Mike, put the bracelets on her—we won't take any chances. Bill, tell the boys on guard no one gets by—or out—get me? No one. Mr. Cornua if you make the slightest move, you will regret it."

Mike snapped a pair of handcuffs on Mary's wrists. She wept bitterly and invoked all the saints of the calendar.

"Mike, search him," and Killark jerked his thumb at me.

"This is an outrage, I protest—"

But the businesslike Mike cut me short by jerking me out of my chair to my feet.

"Bring in that chauffeur and valet outside, Bill. We'll round up the whole crowd."

Mike ran his hands deftly over the outside of my clothes and when he was confident I carried no weapon, proceeded more leisurely to turn out my pockets.

"Here you are, chief. Empty wallet, visiting cards, lady's photygraft, watch, gold Swiss, platinum chain, couple of door keys, pen knife, seventy cents—'s' all."

"Let's see the picture," and Killark took the photograph of Julia's mother that I had found in Howard Birmingham's watch.

"Who is she?" he asked me.

"I refuse to answer."

"Then I'll find out for myself. Let's look at the watch, Mike."

He compared the size of the photograph with the open case of my watch.

"By ginger, Mike, they don't fit. This picture's too big—it comes from somewhere else. Better tell and save trouble, Mr. Cornua."

"No, I can't."

"Have it your own way. Yes, Mike, I think I would, under the circumstances."

This last statement referred to Mike's gesture toward my wrists with another pair of handcuffs. They were clicked into place and for the first time in my life, I, Robert Cornua, millionaire student of philosophy, found myself under arrest and treated like a common criminal suspected of murder. And the worst of it was that I was helpless to give the true explanation even if it would be listened to. I had gone too far now in defense of Julia to turn back. I might as well go on, so I sat in grim silence, my manacled hands in my lap, while Killark resumed his questioning of Mary.

"Ever see this photo, Mary?" and he held out the picture in his hand.

"No, but it's Miss Julia's mother. She's got a big picture of her on her dresser."

Mr. Killark whistled and nodded. He put the photograph away carefully in an inside pocket.

"As Shakespeare says, when in Denmark look for the woman," said Mr. Killark with the air of a man delivering a well-known aphorism.

"How long have you been Miss Gorland's maid, Mary?"

"Six months."

"The pearls the first job you've done in this house?"

"I tell you—"

"Cut that, Mary. Did Mr. Cornua or Grierson find them in your trunk?"

"Jerry—the butler planted them there—the low, snooping hound."

"Now, you said something about finding Mr. Birmingham's body. What did you mean?"

"I was kind of suspicious like when Miss Julia and Mr. Cornua told me Mr. Birmingham had dropped dead—he was an unusually healthy man for his age—and then when Mr. Cornua brought two strangers into the house—I saw them over the top floor banisters—instead of sending for Mr. Birmingham's own doctor—"

"Wait a minute, Mary. Two strangers?"

"Yes, they're upstairs now."

"For the love of Pete—Bill, go get 'em."

"Yes, sir."

"Go on, Mary."

"I can explain all this—" I cut in.

"I don't want to hear it," snapped Killark. "You had your chance and lied. Now you can wait."

It has been my experience that when a person of inferior breeding calls a gentleman a liar there is no use in descending to the level of the accuser by making a heated retort, so I kept silent.

"Now, Mary."

"So being suspicious and all, as I said, and not liking the looks of things at all, at all, I tiptoes down the stairs and squints through Miss Julia's keyhole—which it's God's truth I wouldn't have done, not to save me life, if Miss Julia and Mr. Cornua had not gone out, leaving them two strangers behind—for I'm not one to spy on the lady I works for. Let her do as she likes in her own rooms is Mary Dooggin's motto—but this was different. Leaving two strangers in there and Miss Julia's lingerie scattered all over the place, like she always leaves it—well, there was something funny about that, and besides, it wasn't decent—not that I care for meself, but Miss Julia's a lady—whatever you can say for her friends. I'll take my oath on that—a lady—and as for snitching her pearls—well, I've told you Jerry planted them—"

"Never mind the pearls. What did you see through the keyhole?"

"I saw them two strangers—so help me, Hannah—bending over Mr. Birmingham's body and carrying it out of the room."

"That'll do for the present, Mary. Take her away, Mike. I may need her again—don't load her into the wagon."

"Well, Mr. Cornua, the items in your explanation are beginning to pile up. I hope you can think of all of them."

"My dear Chief," I said, "if you would only stop following clues and listen to facts for a moment, the thing would be simple."

"As I'm not likely to hear any facts I'll stick to my clues, my dear Mr. Cornua. Hullo—what's this?"

Mr. Killark's exclamation was caused by the entrance of the detective Bill, who shoved into the room, a hand on the shoulder of each Mr. Joe Smats and Doctor Tommy.

"Well, Joe," said Mr. Killark, "I guess you've overstepped at last. They all do, Joe. Remember, I warned you last time the magistrate let you off for lack of evidence. I told you then I would get you—and here you are with bells on. Laugh this off, will you?"

"I want to talk over the phone to my lawyer," said Mr. Smats, very sulkily.

"You bet you do. But you aren't going to. Who's your friend there? I don't know his face."

"I am Dr. Thomas Billingworth—here is my card," said Tommy trying to step forward but Bill jerked him back.

"Thanks," said Killark, "but I don't need the services of that kind of a doctor just now. So you've tied up with a young cub doctor, Joe, to help you in your dirty work?"

"I demand my constitutional rights—my lawyer," Joe Smats growled.

"Your constitutional rights are worth right now just one Chinese cent with a hole in it. Joe, you know me, and you know I mean business when it's murder. This is a double murder, get me? So come clean."

"A double murder? What the hell!" exclaimed Tommy.

"So you thought it was only a single one, eh?" said Killark. "Glad you agree to that much. There's the other—on the sofa."

"The butler," Tommy cried in genuine amazement.

"Yes," replied the chief. "His death has been a surprise to everybody. Now then, Joe, you know as well as I do that we'll save a lot of time if us two professionals talk this thing over. I'm sick of asking these amateurs questions."

"Well, Chief," said Mr. Smats rubbing his chin, "I gotta admit I'm in this thing as an amachoor myself—that's why you've got me backed up against the wall. It's kinda humiliatin' for a man of my age and experience to get sucked in like this and I feel it, Chief. I'd feel a little easier if I could talk to my lawyer."

"Nothing doing."

"I got a pretty good defence, Chief, for my share in this."

"I didn't say you hadn't. What I want to know is what happened? How did you get into this?"

"Well, Chief, I didn't think there was a chance any of this Park Avenue crowd—folks that were the real thing—was pulling off any real stuff—just some kind of a stock market job or somethin' legitimate like that—so when Tom here—he's a good boy, Chief—a young doctor—hard-working and stands in with Sid Moroony—don't forget that, Chief—well, when Tom called up and said there was easy Park Avenue money on a thing that was straight but had to be quiet—and they would pay for the quiet—why I fell for it like any hick from Second Avenue. I guess that's all I got to say, Chief, now—until I see my lawyer."

"I take it they were in a hurry to bury Mr. Birmingham?"

"That's about it, Chief."

"Murder?"

"Well, that's more'n you can expect me to talk about without advice of counsel."

"Truss him up, Mike."

"It's humiliatin'," protested Mr. Smats as Mike handcuffed him.

"The doc too, Mike."

"Sure thing," replied Mike, the only words I had heard him utter this evening.

"I'll sue you for false arrest," roared Tommy.

"Like hell," was the Chief's comment on this.

"The newspaper boys outside want to know if you've got any word for them, Chief," said a policeman, coming into the room and saluting.

"Not yet," replied the Chief. "Tell 'em a big story is going to break—early afternoon editions."

"O.K., Chief," said the policeman, and returned whence he came.

"Mike, I leave you in charge—I'm going upstairs and look things over. Come along, Bill—bring your finger print stuff—got everything?"

"I ain't a child, Chief," said Bill in a hurt tone of voice.

At the very instant Mr. Killark, followed by Bill, was about to leave the study, Julia burst in the door almost knocking the detective over with the unexpectedness of her sudden entrance.

"Bobbie," she cried, "something must be done about the servants. They are all weeping and wailing at the top of the house and making a terrible racket!"

Then she saw that we were all handcuffed.

"What's all this, Mr. Detective?" she said, whirling on the still surprised Mr. Killark. "Don't be silly—take those things off Cousin Robert at once."

"Sorry, miss," said the Chief uneasily, "can't be done."

"What do you think you know anyway? Coming into a house in this high handed way and making a fool of yourself—I can prove Mr. Cornua was in his apartment on Park Avenue the whole afternoon and didn't come here until I brought him this evening."

"Steady, Julia," I said.

"Shut your face or I'll quiet you with a nightstick," remarked Mike to me without any malice in his tone.

"Just what I said, men," said Mr. Killark appealing to his staff, who nodded approval, "we won't get any place until we hear this young woman's story."

"I prefer to tell it," said Julia, taking command of the situation, "only in the presence of you and Mr. Cornua."

"Gotta have a stenographer," objected Killark.

"All right, if you've got a reliable one."

"Sure. Tim, forward. The rest of you take Joe, Mary and the Doc into another room and wait orders. Mike, you hold the door. Don't let those newspaper boys pull off anything, Bill."

"First of all, I want you to know Bobbie—Mr. Cornua—is absolutely innocent—he came into this to help me."

Bless her pretty little self, I thought as I looked at her standing defiantly before the detective, her eyes blazing and her cheeks flushed with anger at the outrage of my handcuffs. I thought then and I think now that she was the most beautiful thing I have ever seen.

I trembled for the revelation about her mother that might come to her out of this—perhaps not only grief but the shattering of an illusion, and it is always tragic to see disillusionment come to the young. And I feared that Julia's story might incriminate her in the eyes of a stupid world—her desperate need for money—for such a huge sum as one hundred and fifty thousand dollars under threat of blackmail—and the fact that she was alone in the house when the murder of Howard Birmingham had been committed—that she was Howard's sole heir, consequently the only person who had anything to gain by his death at this time—and yet, I felt that even the unromantic Chief Detective could not look at this beautiful child and believe her guilty. I decided, therefore, to utter no word of protest or warning, but to let Julia tell what she would.

She poured the story forth in the torrent of phrases that serve Julia for sentences when she is excited and I saw with growing delight that Mr. Killark was getting more and more impressed. He listened without a single interruption and I knew why he did that.

He was weighing and comparing every detail, on the look out for the slightest slip or inconsistency—for any trifle that did not make a perfect fit. When Julia had finished, he shoved his felt hat still further back on his head.

"Well, I'm damned," was his first comment. "Mike!" he said, going to the door, "send out and get the headwaiter at the Garden of Aphrodite—Sergius Sagerloop, the Swedish prince, he called himself there—he's Michael Wort, wholesale liquor dealer—quick—general alarm if necessary. Sic the newspaper boys on him too. We've got to get him!"

"O.K., Chief," Mike's voice replied, as Killark shut the door again.

"He's probably made his getaway by now. It's five fifteen now—he's had over five hours, thanks to your amateur detective work, Mr. Cornua," and he unlocked my handcuffs, this act being the first definite indication that he had believed Julia's story. "Of course, you realize you only had yourself to blame for these?" he went on, dangling the handcuffs under my nose.

"Quite right, Chief. No apology is necessary."

"And none is forthcoming—of all the fatheads—I beg your pardon, Miss Gorland—but when I might have nailed a big gang, if I'd been here quick—it makes me sick. We may never get 'em now—thanks to Mr. Cornua's taking the case for his own amusement."

"He did it for me—and what any gentleman would," said Julia hotly.

"Well, all I can say is I'm sorry he's a gentleman. Let's go upstairs and look around—what ought to have been done hours ago. I guess I'll have to ask you to come along, too, Miss Gorland."

"Why of course, I'm not the fainting kind, you know, Mr. Killark. It really isn't done any more."

We climbed the stairs to Julia's dressing-room.

"The next time you are in trouble," Mr. Killark continued, "take my tip. Call in the police and leave your gentleman friend out."

He kneeled and examined the carpet when we showed him where we had found the body.

"Only a small bloodstain—internal hemorrhage did it—or else Joe's done a pretty good clean-up job" he mused, and turned over the manicure knife thoughtfully. I had handed it to him the first thing.

Mr. Killark repeated the search of the room and on examination of the window and outside light much as I had done it earlier that evening.

"I suppose you've carefully mussed up every fingerprint in the place?" asked Mr. Killark, continuing the note of sarcasm which now distinguished all his remarks to me.

"I was careful to wear gloves and to open all doors and window catches without touching the usual places on knobs and fastenings," I replied haughtily.

"It would have been more like sense if you had left this little manicure knife alone. You know," he said weighing it in his hand, "it takes some strength to drive a little thing like this into a man— and you've got to get close enough to do it."

"The exact conclusions I reached earlier."

"Thank you."

He went to the stairs.

"Up here, Bill. Have a look around for fingerprints and—" Bill came up the stairs three at a bound—"and take up this piece of carpet with the blood stain. Have it analyzed."

"Sure thing," replied Bill, and set to work without further comment.

"You couldn't ease the feelings of Mr. Smats and the young doctor by removing their handcuffs, could you?" I asked the Chief.

"Not yet," he replied grimly, "and don't flatter yourself too far just now, Mr. Cornua. We haven't finished."

Mr. Killark's next move was to make a most thorough examination of Howard Birmingham's body. Julia stood with her back turned while this was done, for the detective rejected my suggestion that Julia and I wait outside.

"Whoever killed Mr. Birmingham was either panic stricken or in a frenzy of rage," he said thoughtfully. "Nothing else accounts for the strength needed to drive that little manicure knife through a stiff shirt and the natural resistance of the body. Our problem is this: who might have been frightened enough to do it, or who hated him enough? At first, I thought this was going to link up obviously enough with your blackmailing friend—but what did the black-mailer stand to gain by this job when he had good reason to think you could raise the money for him, Miss Gorland?"

"Perhaps Mr. Birmingham was killed in order to make sure that Miss Gorland could command large sums of money?" I suggested.

"Not a chance. I take it she was only afraid to tell her uncle about her stock gambling?"

"That's true, Mr. Killark. I couldn't tell Uncle Howard I had been such an utter idiot."

"Then there's the crowd outside in the taxi that shot the but-ler. Who were they waiting to get? Not him—what good was a dead butler to them? The other limousine of course was Joe Smats' car—he never goes anywhere without a bodyguard—so we can forget that particular auto—and you, Mr. Cornua, account for your Packard, chauffeur and valet—did you say his name is Evans?"

"Yes."

"And the chauffeur is Martin?"

"Yes."

"Does your valet always carry a Colt automatic?"

"No—I gave it to him before we went to the Garden of Aphrodite tonight."

"Now Miss Garland, can you give me a good description of your stockbroker friend—the fellow who coaxed you into these so-called investments?"

"You mean Toby—or Dudley Flurrel."

"Yes, although that name doesn't mean anything. He probably has a dozen or more."

"Well, I'm rather ashamed of falling a little for Toby now I think it over. You know, Bobbie—I *am* just a little silly with an attractive man."

I nodded with an inward groan. The list of Julia's vacuous-headed dancing companions struck me as appalling, but why com-plain if children like candy?

"He is dark with a sort of movie-hero face and the most charm-ing manners—European, Frieda called them. Always bowed and picked up things for you and kissed your hand."

"Old stuff, eh?" Killark asked.

"It's the old stuff that always tastes best," said Julia demurely. "At any rate, meeting him at Frieda's and all—she's fearfully particular—not modern at all about such things—there must be all kinds of introductions—well I took for granted anyone in her set belonged. I never knew a bounder to slip one over on Frieda. And Toby's manners would please an archbishop—piercing brown eyes, clean cut jaw, nose like a Roman emperor, and all his clothes direct from London, always exactly right—nothing overdone—nothing flashy—no jewelry, except of course cigarette cases and things like that."

"Did you ever go to the Garden of Aphrodite with him?"

"Heavens, no. I only go slumming with Bobbie here to protect me. Of course, Toby and I used to have tea at the Ritz sometimes—but usually we met only at Frieda's parties."

"You never noticed the headwaiter at the Aphrodite joint did you?"

"We all knew he sang over the radio sometimes, accompanied by the orchestra—but I'd never really seen him close to until Bobbie gave him the package with the hundred and fifty thousand dollars in it tonight."

"May I ask, Mr. Cornua, why you did that damn fool thing?"

"I'd do anything to protect Julia—when she is out slumming," I said.

"Bobbie, you are rather a dear you know," exclaimed Julia, suddenly kissing the spot on the top of my head where the hair is growing thin. I was rather embarrassed, considering that Mr. Killark's unromantic eye was upon me.

"Your cash payment," he said coldly, "has financed the whole gang and made their getaway easy. But the thing we've got to worry about is that we can't prove any motive for murder that hitches up with the blackmailers. In fact, Miss Gorland, I am going to have my troubles with the district attorney when I try to explain your actions and those of Mr. Cornua. Especially those of Mr. Cornua. Being a damn fool is not a good legal defence."

"I shall consult my lawyers in the morning," I said with dignity.

"I should, if I were you—they'll give you an earful when they hear what you did—meanwhile I am likely to be of more assistance to you—only don't forget this, Mr. Cornua, I still have to consider the obvious theory until I get something nearer the truth. You have a motive—to secure a fortune for Miss Gorland—and your actions in calling in a strange doctor, in getting rid of the family physician, and sending for Joe Smats, one of the biggest uncaught crooks in New York, haven't helped you a bit,. Then there is the photograph business—"

"What is that?" asked Julia.

"I'm not going to bring that up now," said Killark, responding to the slight gesture I made. "The best I can do for you, Mr. Cornua, is to persuade the office to let you out on bail."

"Are you going to charge me?"

"Bobbie, he can't. It's too silly! Think of your alibi."

"Just listen to me for a minute, folks. Don't forget the newspapers—especially the tabloids. Now those boys aren't going to overlook the obvious theory—and you can imagine what they will say about the police if I don't make the obvious arrests. I'm awfully sorry about this—on your account. Miss Gorland—because it's going to be pretty tough publicity for you to face—but I've got an idea you've got nerve and can stand it. The only way I can possibly save this situation and find out who killed Howard Birmingham is to arrest you—and your friend, Mr. Cornua, and to hold your doctor and Joe Smats. As for Mary—"

"Mary?" queried Julia in surprise.

"Your maid Eloise," explained Mr. Killark. "She's got a string of your pearls in the bottom of her trunk, so that fixes her nicely for me."

"Oh, but you mustn't arrest Eloise! Do be reasonable. I can't do without her."

"She admits she has your pearls."

"Poor thing. You must have frightened her into doing it."

"What, stealing?"

"No, telling about it. What do I care if she did? She's the best maid I ever had—what does the Bible say about a pearl without price? Be charitable, Mr. Killark."

"Can't be done with Mary, but I'll hold up the charge until I'm sure I don't find her mixed up in this thing."

"Eloise! How preposterous!"

"Well, Miss Gorland, if you'll pardon my saying so, your judgment of human nature hasn't turned out infallible"—Mr. Killark gave me a hard look—"and this maid of yours has acted suspiciously. You see, there must be some link inside this house with the outside. That's the first thing to locate."

"How about the other servants?"

"Horace is questioning them now. He'll report soon."

"Horace?" asked Julia.

"One of my experts on the Homicide Squad—Horace Innesfree."

With this Mr. Killark led the way back to the study. It was now six minutes after six and growing broad daylight outside. For fifteen minutes he was busy on the telephone. Finally he hung up after giving various instructions and repeating Julia's description of Dudley Flurrel. Grierson's body had been taken away during our absence.

"We'll ship your doctor, Joe and Mary off in the wagon and any others Horace says to hold—that'll send most of the newspaper boys hotfooting it after them. You, Miss Gorland, and Mr. Cornua will ride downtown with me in Mr. Cornua's Packard after you've had time to dress and brush up, Miss Gorland. Mr. Cornua, you had better stop on the way at your apartment and get your week-end bag, just in case you are detained."

"If Bobbie goes to jail, I go with him," said Julia firmly.

"You won't help him that way, Miss Gorland. You will be more use to him working with me to identify Dudley Flurrel, if we have the luck to pick him up—and the head waiter. Besides, I've got a nice little collection of photographs I want you to look over. Perhaps you can spot Dudley Flurrel in the rogue's gallery."

Another plainclothes man whom I had not noticed before entered the room.

"What's the news, Horace?" asked Killark.

"Other servants O.K. Bunch of scared boobs. The taxi that was outside has been found deserted on Pelham Parkway. Number plates on it from another taxi stolen last week in New Rochelle. No clues—no fingerprints in taxi."

"All right, Horace. Take charge here, I'm sending Mike and Bill with the wagon. You're checking up on who Grierson was?"

"Fred's upstairs going through his things and will follow up any leads he gets."

"O.K., Horace."

The detective nodded and left the room.

# VII
## THE DISTRICT ATTORNEY INVESTIGATES

I ANTICIPATED MY INTERVIEW in the district attorney's office was not a pleasant one, but I will give Chief Detective Killark credit for standing my friend in spite of the suspicions of the shrewd legal mind who heard my story.

"The only thing that makes me think you are on the right track in this case, Killark," said the attorney, a cynical young man with premature grey hair, "is that Cornua's story is so damned preposterous that it's probably true. Whatever happened, I certainly don't believe this murder was committed by a jackass."

"That's what I think," said Killark.

I opened my mouth to speak, but thought better of it.

"You're sure it couldn't have been the girl—the niece, I mean?" the attorney continued.

"She hasn't the physical strength."

"Haven't I seen her name in the papers as playing in golf and tennis tournaments? Swimming, too—and fancy diving. Don't forget Killark, girls aren't what they were when you were a boy."

"It's more than a hunch—I know she didn't do it."

"She was panic stricken over the money involved in the black-mail mess."

"Yes, she was scared—like a kid expecting a spanking for getting scratched pulling the cat's tail. You can't find any murder motive in her. She was stuck on this uncle, who spoiled her and gave her everything she wanted before she asked for it."

"Except that she was afraid to ask him for a hundred and fifty thousand dollars."

"That never really worried her. She knew this man here, Cornua, would come across for her any time."

"Why did you give her the one hundred and fifty thousand dollars, Mr. Cornua? Had you ever given her large sums before?" The attorney turned to me.

"No—little presents on her birthday and at Christmas, of course. I was Howard Birmingham's most intimate friend and thought as much of his niece as he did."

"So that's why you passed out all that money—without stopping to think?"

"I did think. I wanted to protect her name whatever it cost."

"Did you ever propose marriage to her?"

"No, certainly not. Look at the discrepancy in our ages. I was just another member of the family to her."

"About this photograph, Mr. Cornua, which you very injudiciously removed—you say—from Mr. Birmingham's watch. Why did you do it?"

"Great heavens, man, I've told you it is a picture of Julia's mother. I didn't want her to know of it—to have any suspicions—to think things either about her mother—or the man she thought was her uncle."

"You say you did not know her alleged father and real mother—Yes, I see here in my notes you've answered that. You know nothing about either of them—of Gorland, himself, for example?"

"I wish I did, for I have an idea, Mr. Attorney, that if we could lay our hands on Mr. Gorland we might solve this mystery."

"You don't believe he is dead, then? Have you any reason for thinking this?"

"Only that Grierson, the butler, evaded my questions about this—and seemed to know something he would not tell."

"Then you do not believe that the blackmailer and the murderer of Mr. Birmingham are the same?"

"I think they are two separate problems—that only coincidence brought them together on the same day—that possibly Howard's murder was a vengeance long planned—the other, a plot by a common confidence man to extort money from Miss Gorland."

"Which party killed Grierson then?"

"I don't know."

"Killark," said the attorney, "some gunmen were waiting to shoot down some one who was expected to leave Mr. Birmingham's house in the middle of the night. And yet the blackmail had been paid, and Mr. Cornua had come and gone with Miss Gorland unmolested. You saw the taxi across the street, you said, Mr. Cornua."

"Yes."

"And didn't report it to the police?"

"I've explained why twice. I thought it was part of the blackmailing gang checking up on whether we had taken the money to the Garden of Aphrodite—that when they saw us come back again, they would go away."

"Who did they expect would leave the house in the middle of the night? And why did they expect he would leave at such an hour?"

"That part of this case beats me, Mr. Attorney," said Killark.

"The gunmen in the taxi did not know that Mr. Birmingham was already dead," said the district attorney, putting his fingertips together. "Were there two plots afoot to murder this millionaire?"

"It's got me dippy, Mr. Attorney."

"There must have been some message delivered to Mr. Birmingham of such a nature that he was expected to answer it by leaving his house in the middle of the night. Now what kind of message could it have been that they could confidently expect he would obey? I take it, Mr. Cornua, that you would have been surprised to have Mr. Birmingham call alone at your apartment in the middle of the night? He did not go abroad much then, I imagine?"

"Never. He lived an extremely retired life and when Julia wanted to go out to late parties, it was usually I who took her."

"But before he could answer the message, he was murdered in his own house—and the gunmen outside *did not know it*, or they would not have shot down the butler in mistake for Mr. Birmingham."

"That's the way I dope it out, Mr. Attorney."

"It's a complex case, Killark. Mr. Cornua I apologize for the word 'jackass' a few minutes ago. I believe your suggestion to trace Mr. Gorland is the best lead that offers. And allow me to say, sir, that I personally have, for the present, no suspicion of you—but you know the newspapers and their power. I shall therefore have to hold you as a material witness. I do not need to bring any charge against you, and I can arrange for your personal comfort, if you are willing to pay for special food and service, while you are detained. As for your doctor friend, I can let him off, too, after he has given what will of course be damaging testimony against you—testimony that may force me to lay a serious charge against you. But the young doctor, technically, was interrupted before he had an opportunity to commit a crime by issuing a false death certificate."

"I am appreciative of your courtesy and consideration," I said.

"Don't ever again try to take the law into your own hands, Mr. Cornua, or play detective, because I must tell you frankly that if we don't find Mr. Gorland, the case against you will become very strong. There is only Miss Julia's alibi for you—and to use that would involve her since she would then become the only person known to have been in Mr. Birmingham's house when he was killed. Keep cool, Mr. Cornua. I shall do my best. And don't talk to the reporters—not that I shall allow any of them to see you—but don't issue statements to the press through your attorneys or any other agent."

After some more wearisome technicalities in the district attorney's office I was allowed to say good-bye to Julia, and found myself at nine twenty-three sitting down in a comfortably furnished cell—really a deluxe affair reserved, as I imagined, for unusual detentions—and facing an excellent breakfast sent in, at my expense, from outside. The events of the night, although they had fatigued me had also made me hungry and I ate my bacon and eggs, rolls and coffee with great gusto.

At nine fifty-two my lawyer arrived, Mr. Eric Casler, senior partner of Casler, Godstrong, Casler and Casler, whose acute advice had guided for many years my investments. He was, as I feared he would be, unutterably distressed over the predicament in which he found me. Never in the seventy years of his firm's existence had one of the clients of this house been under the shadow of a murder-charge. Of course, occasional irregularities in the financial world had brought some unwonted retainers to the office, but in general the firm did business only for the socially impeccable.

Mr. Casler had the bedside manner of an eminent specialist. When he said "tut tut," as he frequently did to the details of my story the tut tut echoed all the way down from his gleaming eye-glasses through his snow white whiskers across an immaculate broadcloth waistcoat piped with a line of white around the black cravat on to the pearl buttons on his grey spats.

"What I simply cannot understand, my dear Mr. Cornua, is why a person of your perspicacity did not consult me over the telephone when you heard Miss Gorland's account of what had happened in Mr. Birmingham's house. I could have been reached at Pierre's where I was dining—I left word at my house, you know—and later when I was in my box at the opera I gave instructions to the ticket-office to notify me immediately if any message came. I am never out of touch—our office is never out of touch—with our clients night or day."

"Of course, I see now that I did not fully realize what I was letting myself in for."

"The law, Mr. Cornua, is never a trifling matter—except possibly a sumptuary law—" and Mr. Eric Casler coughed behind his hand, for he must have recalled giving me an occasional glass of very good Burgundy—"but to take the law into one's own hands—dear me, Mr. Cornua, I can't conceive what you were thinking of. Distressing is the only word that occurs to me."

"Will you take the case?" I asked bluntly.

"Dear me, no. We are not criminal lawyers, Mr. Cornua. I thought you knew we specialized only in corporation law—with a few distinguished private clients like yourself. I can put you in touch, however, with a reliable firm, and shall continue privately to advise you—but dear me, I could not attend you in court. Think of our reputation, Mr. Cornua. Have you seen these deplorable extras?" and Mr. Casler unfolded a vivid illustrated newspaper. From a huge headline in block letters across the top carrying the announcement "Millionaire Murdered!" my eyes travelled to a photograph of a young woman in what is called I believe for politeness' sake, lingerie.

"A composite photograph, it is entitled," explained Mr. Casler, "it shows the interior of Mr. Birmingham's drawing room from an actual photograph, and the picture of the young woman in the—er—ah—underthings has been superimposed upon it. The inscription beneath reads as follows—yes." He adjusted his glasses and read: "'Niece of the slain man, Miss Gorland, as she often appeared in her boudoir. Posed by Miss Billee Bettina of the Dionysian Revels. Lingerie by Soijambe Corp., Fifth Avenue,' and that, Mr. Cornua, sir, is modern journalism. Bah," and Mr. Casler smote the picture with the back of his hand. "Here, on the next page, you will find a floor plan of Mr. Birmingham's house with a cross marking the spot where the body was found, and two headlines 'Will Cornua Talk?' and 'How Much Does Julia Know?' Below is the information that you are being held incommunicado at police headquarters."

"That, at least, is true," I said.

"I must bid you good morning for the time being, Mr. Cornua, but I shall keep in close touch. The district attorney has promised me a brief conference with him. I shall try to make him see your error as an act of folly, sir—one committed by a layman's ignorance of the law."

"I believe he already has described it as an act of folly," I said.

"A lawyer would inevitably see it that way—and yet, Mr. Cornua, that does not excuse us from the results of our folly. It becomes now in part my task to rescue you from the gravest of these possible consequences. From some things that you have done you cannot be absolved. But I trust—I sincerely trust—we can prevent a conviction for first degree—or if not, that we may be successful on an appeal. But it is my duty to warn you that you stand in great danger."

With these reassuring words Mr. Casler took his leave. After he had gone I read every word of the lurid account of the mysterious double murder. Grierson's as was natural, was regarded as only a spicy addition to the details. And through every paragraph ran not only the insinuation of my guilt but the much more disturbing insinuations about Julia's relation to the affair. "Was Cornua Julia's sugar daddy?" was a query I found heading a whole column of innuendo.

The very thing I had striven for, to save Julia from the slightest breath of scandal, had failed; yet if Grierson had not been shot down, I would have succeeded in concealing the true cause of Howard Birmingham's death, the blackmail paid and no one would have known a single fact. I cared little for the consequences so far as I was concerned. At forty-five one begins to become fatalistic, but the pain I felt for Julia was deep and sincere. Never have I in all my life met a better and a more lovable woman, and I had known her from childhood, had always in fact thought of her as a child up until the events of the night. I realized now that she was a woman and would suffer as a woman in this horrible enigma.

It would not be long, of course, before she would find out about her mother—but what? What was the secret there? Was Gorland a man who had made life intolerable for his wife? Was it he who had returned after all these years to strike Howard Birmingham down? But making all the excuses for Julia's mother I could, I had also to remember there had been a Mrs. Birmingham and that it was not his wife's picture that I had found in the case of Howard's watch. Whatever Gorland had been to his wife, she had to bear some guilt—or was there an explanation none of us had guessed? Was I only building up without any foundation a mass of innuendo in my own mind—like the filthy imaginings of the newspaper that lay in my lap? This thought gave me pause. "Find Gorland!" I exclaimed aloud. "The answer is with him!"

# VIII
## JULIA'S DAY

I MUST DROP MY PART in this narrative for the time being since my incarceration, or rather detention, as a material witness made it impossible for me to share in the next events. I am obliged therefore to allow Julia to continue the story in her own words as I took them down subsequently. I think an unbiased reader will discover Julia to be an accurate observer and a vivacious reporter, although it is not always easy to follow the sequence of her thought.

"Bobbie, of course I was absolutely desolate to leave you in that terrible place—with bars on the windows and everything—but Charlie—that's the name of the nice district attorney who believed us and let me off—Charlie said you would be quite comfortable and could have your own chef if you wanted him—I do hope you ate properly because it is so important to keep up one's strength at such a time—and strange cooking puts one off so—then Charlie took me back to Uncle Howard's house with Mr. Killark and a whole flock of cops on motor cycles with screaming sirens—just as if I was Lindbergh or one of Grover Whalen's friends—and there were hundreds of cameras and newspaper men trying to ask things—but Charlie waved them all aside and the police pushed them back—and I worried a little about the cameras because I dressed so hurriedly this morning—naturally I wasn't thinking of such things just after Uncle Howard's death and I didn't have Eloise to help me—and she's such a good judge of effect—so I expect I shall look an awful fright in the rotogravure sections—and people will say a thing that looks like that must be guilty of something—quite the criminal

96

type—but Charlie was firm from the first that there was nothing to worry about—that he had lines out all over the place—and nothing could escape his dragnet—and a lot more to the same effect.

"Don't tell Charlie I said so, because he's been awfully nice, but he gets just a little above himself now and then—self-confidence, I expect.

"Well, who should I find sitting on the door step of the house but Billy—of course the police wouldn't let him in—and he had spent the night in a cell because he did quarrel with that traffic officer after we left him—and he was fined twenty-five dollars and costs for telling the traffic officer a few home truths—but it was worth it every cent, Billy said—and he would have had another row with the police in Uncle Howard's house only they had slammed the door in his face and left him outside. He told me he had vowed not to move until he saw me again—and it would have been terrible if I had been arrested too and not come back, for Billy might have sat there until he starved to death.

"Charlie—that's the district attorney, Oh, I've said that before— Charlie wasn't a bit pleased to find Billy there and was going to wave him away and have him pushed by motorcycle cops which would have started something again with Billy, only I finally persuaded Charlie I needed all my friends and he let Billy stay. He said it wasn't right for outsiders to speak to a material witness— he meant me—so Billy had to hang around on the horizon, so to speak. In fact, Charlie made that big tall fellow with the red hair called Mike—you remember him, of course—he told Mike to be Billy's escort and go everywhere with him—which made Billy a little ratty because he was fed up on police. But I calmed Billy down with a look and he offered Mike a cigarette. I don't know why but Mike said something very rude about cigarettes—Charlie explained that Mike only smoked cigars—men are so funny.

"We left Billy and Mike downstairs—and Billy was showing Mike a few simple card tricks—while I took Charlie and Mr. Killark all over the house—top to bottom—kitchens, attic—everything. Uncle Howard had been taken away—Grierson too, of course. It was pretty hard of course—there were so many things to remind one—and only yesterday—and then yesterday seemed millions of years ago—and the world had changed so in the meantime it could never be the same—and I cried a little—and you know, Bobbie, I'm not the crying kind—I was glad Billy was downstairs—and Charlie was very nice and turned his back and all—never even said 'there, there, little girl'—which a stupid man would have done.

"Charlie made a great many notes and he and Killark talked together a great deal in whispers—and he wouldn't let me see his notes—said they were technical—then he surprised me very much by asking if he could take mother's photograph away with him— the big one in the silver frame on my dresser, you know, Bobbie.

"'Whatever for?' I asked him.

"'You will have to trust me and believe I have a good reason,' he said. 'I'll take the greatest possible care of it and see you get it back safely.'

"Well, of course I didn't like it and I couldn't understand then why he was so mysterious about it—but I couldn't very well say 'no,' because he could take it anyway if he wanted to, so I said 'yes— but I hold you personally responsible for returning it just as soon as possible.' He promised and I let him have it.

"Then he surprised me some more by saying that we were now going over to see Frieda Minters and talk to her about Dudley Flurrel. I explained it wouldn't be a bit of use because Frieda never got up before noon and that her temper was impossible until she had had her bath and her aspirin, but Charlie insisted and I had to telephone her we were coming—and Frieda sounded very cross at the other end, just as I expected, but she said if we were coming she supposed we'd have to come.

"We left Billy behind with Mike—he seemed quite happy because Mike took a real interest in the card tricks and Billy had always had a hard time finding a good audience for his stuff—and drove over to Frieda's apartment with the motorcycle escort as before—to keep off the reporters, Charlie said. It was fun to go sailing right through traffic lights and everything and not hear a word— only salutes—made one feel frightfully important.

"Frieda received us in that new negligee of hers she just got from Paris—she really looks very well in it—only it's a trifle risqué; at least considering she had never met Charlie before. If you know Frieda well you get used to her not wearing very much—but at first, it might be misunderstood, you know.

"I noticed at once that Frieda seemed to draw into her shell when she found what we had come for. It was all a great surprise to her because she hadn't seen the morning paper. Charlie began questioning her right off.

"'When did you first meet the man who calls himself Dudley Flurrel?' he asked.

"'About—six months ago,' said Frieda in her snooty voice that she keeps for people who don't belong. She seemed to take an instinctive dislike to poor Charlie.

"'Where?'

"'I can't recall—Oh, yes—I met him at a private dance—he seemed rather a pleasant person—so I asked him to drop in to tea one day. He came quite often after his first call.'

"'Do you know anything about him really? Did you every make any inquiries about him?'

"'I didn't think it necessary. He went everywhere—and everyone believed he was on the Street—with some big house—he played an excellent game of contract—and was most useful. He was always willing to fill in at parties—even at the last moment.'

"'That seems to indicate that he did not have many engagements—everywhere.'

"'I really never gave the matter a thought until Julia told me of her experience with him. Of course I dropped him at once and haven't seen him since.'

"'Did you ever invest any money through him?'

"'No. I have a sufficient income.'

"'You play contract for rather large stakes, I believe?'

"'Is that really any of your business?'

"'I don't know, Miss Minters. Perhaps. Did you win any money from Dudley Flurrel?'

"'Aren't you rather impertinent?'

"'I am afraid that is my business, Miss Minters. Please answer my question.'

"'Why should I?'

"'Because Miss Minters, the man with whom you have been associating has proved himself a criminal—and because a double murder has been committed with which this man may or may not be connected. Under these circumstances I have the power to compel you to answer my questions—but I prefer to put them and to have them answered in a friendly spirit. I advise you, therefore, to change the tone of your replies.'

"'I see. You threaten me, in other words.'

"'I must have answers.'

"Frieda gave Charlie a dirty look at this, but he kept his eyes on hers without batting them once, and she gave way.

"'Dudley Flurrel was usually my partner at contract. Yes—we did win some fairly large sums. He was a good player, as I have said—and I've made something of a study of the game myself. One naturally enjoys playing with a good partner.'

"'And winning, Miss Minters.'

"'Well, yes—and winning. One usually plays games to win, if one can.'

"'Are the winnings of contract-bridge an important part of your income?'

"'I—I—yes, I suppose they are.'

"'Why did you advise Miss Gorland to play the stock market through Dudley Flurrel?'

"'Well, Julia owed me a lot. I let her play because I knew money didn't matter much to her—after all, her uncle was one of the richest men in New York—why shouldn't she play if she wanted to? Then when she said she owed more than her allowance and didn't dare to tell her uncle about her losses, because of his strict views on gambling—I suggested the market to her. Everyone was doing it—it was what is called a bull market—and things were going up and up. Hundreds of my friends were making heaps of money—why shouldn't Julia?'

"'You suggested Dudley Flurrel as broker?'

"'Yes—we thought he was something on the Street—he said so—and Julia knew him. There was no risk of her uncle finding out if she dealt through a friend.'

"'I see. Were you quite ethical, Miss Minters?'

"'Good grief, this is New York, not heaven. Julia has been out one season. She's not a child.'

"'And yet, with this splendid opportunity, you didn't try to make any money in the market yourself?'

"'I stick to the game I know.'

"'One other question, Miss Minters. Did you ever go to the Garden of Aphrodite—it's a night club—with Dudley Flurrel?'

"'Certainly not.'

"'Then you don't know the head waiter at that place?'

"'I've never been inside its doors. It's rather a vulgar place, isn't it? How could you imagine I know anything about the head waiter there?'

"'Thank you. I shall not trouble you further this morning,' Charlie said and rose to his feet.

"I followed him—saying good-bye to Frieda rather coldly because it gave me quite a shock to find how hardboiled she is. After all—to confess making a business of contract—well, there are limits! Frieda murmured something conventional to me about Uncle Howard—and do you know, Bobbie, it didn't occur to me until I got into the car again with Charlie that I still owed Frieda for my losses. You see, Toby's blackmailing—Dudley, you know,—drove everything out of my head about the other debt.

"'I wonder just how much she is lying?' Charlie said to himself as the car moved off.

"I noticed he had spoken to one of his detectives in the entrance of the apartment house when we came out.

"'Are you having her watched?' I asked.

"'You bet I am,' answered Charlie, 'and her past looked up as well. I expect to know a lot more about Miss Frieda Minters by evening. Meanwhile, Julia, you must be worn out, not having had any sleep for twenty-four hours, so I am going to take you back to your uncle's house and order you to go to bed. I can have you guarded there from reporters or any other disturbances. You won't mind staying in the house now, will you? At a hotel the reporters would surely bother you.'

"Of course I was awfully sleepy and tired, though I hadn't stopped to think about it until Charlie mentioned it, and the house wasn't scary, not with all those policemen downstairs. And Charlie promised to let me know just as soon as he had any news, whatever it was, and to wake me up if necessary, so I said 'yes.'"

## IX
## MR. KILLARK'S ADVICE

ON THE FOLLOWING DAY Mr. Killark of the Homicide Squad called upon me, equipped as usual with his tilted felt hat and obese cigar, neither of which had I ever seen him remove except once—and that had been caused by the influence of Julia's presence. As a philosopher I was curious to know why the usual phenomena of smoke, ashes and odor always proceeded from Mr. Killark's cigars, but that otherwise they appeared to stand still in time and space, growing neither shorter nor longer, nor even singeing the gaudy belt of red and gold that encased them. Even the perpetual fire upon the Capitoline Hill at Rome was fed by vestal virgins, but Mr. Killark's cigars must have been lighted by a coal from the everlasting flames of Dis, since they blazed without attendance. In conversation the cigar would roll about in the corner of Mr. Killark's mouth, apparently suffering no other inconvenience than does a swimmer ploughing through waves in the throes of the Australian crawl.

"It's about your friend, Joe Smats," said Mr. Killark through one revolution of the cigar.

"Friend is hardly the exact word," I replied mildly, wondering if Mr. Killark would sense my literary reference to Flaubert.

"Side-kick—racketeer partner—I don't care what you call him, Mr. Cornua. I'm getting more interested in why you two went into this thing. A child in arms would know that Grierson killed Birmingham—."

I started at this because no hint of such a development of the case had been revealed to me by the district attorney.

103

"Sure. But to make a plausible story about it is something else again. I can't prove it. And I don't know why Grierson did it. And I don't know why Grierson was shot. And I'm damned if I know where you and Joe Smats come into this thing. Why, Joe is one of the best boys in town for any fancy racket. It's against nature for him to leave himself wide open like this. I've been trying to get the goods on Joe for ten years and never even got a case that would get beyond a magistrate's desk. And now, here he is. It's too easy, Mr. Cornua—that's what's the trouble. It makes me nervous."

"Too easy?"

"Absopositively. Joe's one wise guy. When he frames up a situation which says 'Here, Killark, arrest me. You've got me cold in a mistake a baby wouldn't make'—why, you see, Mr. Cornua, it's got me buffaloed. There's something back of it. It's a trap to make me look foolish. I won't touch him. I wouldn't charge that guy now even if we'd found the whole Board of Aldermen murdered in his cellar."

"As Virgil says," I ventured, "you fear the Greeks even though bearing gifts."

"Say, I've never been afraid of any Greek yet—not even that guy that had a pineapple farm in his cellar under his fruit-store—"

"Pineapple farm?" I queried. "In a cellar— But they are tropical fruit."

"Not these ain't. Pineapples is handy little bombs, Mr. Cornua. Little greeting packages full of T.N.T."

Mr. Killark, of course, had hopelessly misunderstood my classical allusion, but I feared it would embarrass him to enlighten him.

"Besides," Mr. Killark continued, "Joe Smats ain't no Greek. He's a Connecticut Yankee with a summer home in Westport—and those guys come high, wide, and mean. His wife runs a gift-shop on the Boston Post Road and sells antiques and batik. That gives you some kind of an idea what I'm up against. Now, Mr. Cornua, I've got to have your help. Just put your cards on the table and tell me what it's all about."

"I suppose it is useless for me to insist upon Mr. Smats' innocence? That he was merely inveigled into this thing on, as it were, false pretences?"

"Mr. Cornua, I don't want you to get me wrong—this ain't no insult, but a statement of fact. Any day you could inveigle Joe Smats into being innocent, you could get yourself elected King of Ireland on a prohibition ticket as a Methodist candidate."

"You are at least emphatic."

"You are damn tooting, I am. Look here, Mr. Cornua. You're a good scout, I know that. You got into this mess because you're soft over the girl—that's to your credit. She's a nice kid, I don't blame you. But what I know won't help you, unless I can know more. Get me? I have no evidence that will prove a thing. All the evidence I got points at you and Joe Smats. Sure, I know Grierson did it, but I've no proof. And the newspapers will frame you and Smats if we don't look out. That's my point. Your life is in danger, Mr. Cornua. Just try to get that idea absorbed into your philosophy. Why even now, innocent as you are, the prosecutor would make a monkey of you on cross-examination."

"You appear to me to be inconsistent, Mr. Killark. You believe in my innocence but not in that of Mr. Smats. How do you reconcile this illogicality?"

"I don't think Smats had anything to do with the murder. And I can't make myself believe he would step into this just for your asking. There's another racket in this thing— perhaps it begins in *The Garden of Aphrodite*. Whatever you know about Smats, you don't know all—or much. He must have been wise to the whole blackmail racket, or he wouldn't have come in. Get me?"

"Then what do you want of me?"

"I want you to help me get Joe Smats. I can't touch him now, see? The present layout is an invitation—that means it's phony."

"You place me in a difficult position, Mr. Killark. I feel under deep obligation to Mr. Smats for his assistance and for the fact that he has made no effort to divert your suspicions by turning against me."

"It's his job to fool you, Mr. Cornua. Believe me, he isn't working for your health—or Miss Julia's either—don't forget that. You may think he's your friend—"

"I'm under no illusions about that. I am paying him for what he did for me."

"Yes, and now he's going into business for himself. You've given him the chance of a lifetime to make a big clean-up. Now I want you to seem to play into his hands, see? String him along that you think he's helping you and Miss Julia get out of this. Then keep in touch with me—and we'll see what happens."

"I don't like duplicity, Mr. Killark. They who touch pitch will be defiled."

"You're a good one to talk about duplicity. Trying to conceal a murder and turning cash over to blackmailers I suppose you class as indoor sports. Just cast your eye over this editorial, Mr. Cornua."

I took the paper from his outstretched hand while Mr. Killark shifted the angle of his cigar. Glancing at the page, I read: "The pretence that there is some mystery in the slaying of Howard Birmingham should no longer be maintained. The guilty man, described by our venal police force as only a material witness, sits in security while the gunmen, his minions who shot down the butler Grierson in cold blood, are allowed to stalk about the streets of Manhattan in search of further prey—" and so on for several hundred words. The whole was headed "Arrest Cornua!"

"Something must be done," I said, laying down the paper.

"Now you are whistling," Mr. Killark confirmed.

"If your office will release me, I shall go make a call upon Mr. Joe Smats."

"I've got a closed car waiting outside so you won't be recognized by the reporters on the way. Go to it, but don't try to put anything over on me."

With this benison upon my head from Mr. Killark, I departed. For over twenty-four hours I had been virtually a prisoner at Headquarters. One needs clean linen after such an experience.

# X
## MR. SMATS DECLARES WAR

I STOPPED AT MY PARK AVENUE APARTMENT on the way uptown. Mr. Smats' business address was in a part of the Bronx of which I had never heard, and before going so far afield, I felt that I needed a wash and brush up very badly. One can't go rushing blindly into the Bronx. Evans received me, his eyes more reproachful than ever. After all, it is upsetting to one's valet to have charges of murder bandied about in the public press and poor Evans himself had been none too gently questioned by Mr. Killark's squad of police.

"'Ave they laid 'ands on the culprit, sir?" was his greeting, as I stretched myself for a moment in my familiar armchair, a siphon by my side and pipeful of Latakia between my teeth. It seemed years since I had sat there last.

"I'm sorry to say they haven't, Evans," I replied.

"Quite so, sir. Will you wear an Oxford or a percale? Bow tie, sir?"

"An Oxford, Evans—something quiet, and a four-in-hand, of course. One doesn't—you know—at a time like this."

"Quite, sir, quite," Evans agreed.

"And if that young woman comes who does my typewriting, tell her to get on with the manuscript, will you? And to leave blank the bits she can't read. It's no good her writing Copenhagen when I wrote Schopenhauer—tell her."

"Yes, sir."

In a few minutes Evans had arrayed me in fresh linen and another suit.

"Remember," I said to him as I left, "not a word to the reporters."

"No, sir."

"And call round every day to see if Miss Julia needs anything."

"Yes, sir. But aren't you coming back, sir?"

"One does not know," I replied. "Whether I do or don't, carry on, Evans."

"Certainly, sir," he said, drawing himself up with a recollection of his military training in his bearing.

"Always have a dinner ready for me at the usual time—exactly seven-thirty. I may look in and eat one someday."

"Yes, sir."

The car which had been waiting for me while I made my change was a Headquarters' affair, of course, for Mr. Killark could not allow me complete freedom of action. The chauffeur I knew was a detective of some kind, with orders not to allow me too much rope. It was really rather decent of him not to make a fuss while I had the bath and change.

Mr. Smats lived a long way off. At least, we drove for a long time through a part of the city it had never been my lot to visit before. We passed an incredible number of moving-picture houses, I noted, as well as mysterious elevated railways one had never dreamed of. The Bronx looked like an area that might be fruitfully investigated by a philosopher of human nature.

We paused—and by we, I mean the car, the chauffeur-detective, and I, at least for the moment a unit with the other two, before an extraordinary looking shop-front containing behind huge plate-glass windows enormous palms in gigantic vases—with a gilt sign over the central doorway inscribed "Home from Home," and in another place "Rest and Comfort for the Weary. Complete automobile funerals, no extras, at all one price." I adjusted my shell-rim glasses and stepped to the door, for there were other signs that caught my eye. "Visit our undenominational chapel," I read.

I had a slight difficulty in visualizing Mr. Joe Smats conducting a chapel, undenominational or otherwise.

I stepped through the plate glass revolving door into a long tile-lined corridor of rococo Gothic style, adorned with more palms.

A young woman with intensely yellow hair sat at an ornate desk.

"Is it your poor wife?" she asked with a most sympathetic voice, a tone almost like a melodious birdcall.

I stared at her, because for the life of me I couldn't imagine for a moment what her question meant.

"There—there," she went on, laying a carefully manicured hand reassuringly on my arm. "Take your time. Pull yourself together, sir. I know just how you feel. Won't you sit down? Would you like a glass of ginger ale?"

I sank into a chair wondering if the woman were demented.

"We can do you a lovely thing for five hundred dollars, flowers included," she went on. "Shall I show you some pictures? This is a sample of our bronze eternal."

A great light dawned upon me. The woman thought I had come about a funeral—well, of course, I had in a sense, only not in the way she thought. I laughed. I couldn't help it.

"Don't give way to hysterics, sir. Here, have a drop of this,—it's real brandy."

"Thank you, no," I said. "I've called to see Mr. Joe Smats—on a very important matter."

"Have you an appointment?" she asked suspiciously, her whole manner changing.

"No," I replied, "but if you will tell him who I am, he will see me."

"And who shall I say you are?" she asked, as she fingered a telephone plug on the board by her desk.

"Mr. Robert Cornua," I replied.

She started and it was her turn to stare at me with amazement.

"The Mr. Cornua—of the Birmingham murder?"

I nodded.

"Gee!" was her comment, her eyes, the lids heavy with mascara, opening wide.

I observed that the tabloids had spread such report of me that my very presence struck awe into her soul. Like a woman in a trance, but with her eyes fixed upon my face, she called Mr. Smats' inner sanctum and conveyed to him the information of my arrival.

"He will see you at once, sir," she said, at the end of her consultation over the wire. "Step right inside, second door on the right." Her voice sounded like a person speaking humbly to one of the great ones of earth, and her eyes followed me intently as I passed down Mr. Smats' palm-bedecked hall to the door of his private office.

"Walk right in, Mr. Cornua," he sang out at my respectful tap upon the frosted glass.

I entered to the sudden confusion of another blonde, obviously Mr. Smats' stenographer, who arose with a clatter of pencils and dropped notebooks at the announcement of my name and actual presence.

"'S'all right, Edith," said Mr. Smats reassuringly. The reader must remember that every sensational newspaper in New York had described me, not only as the murderer of Howard Birmingham, but as the master-mind that had destroyed Grierson for knowing too much—the object of all these crimes being my desire to possess the fortune and body of Miss Julia Gorland.

It was of interest to me, as a philosopher of human nature, that Mr. Smats was able so exactly to duplicate his taste in blondes with the young woman he called Edith, who might easily pass, at a hasty glance, for the twin of the girl at the entrance switchboard. They were both, in fact what one might call undulatory blondes—that is, their every movement set their hips swaying.

"It is now eleven thirty-six, Mr. Smats," I began, dismissing momentarily the problem of duplicate blondes, "and I am rather pressed for time. May I see you in private?" and I tried delicately to gesture that I regarded Miss Edith—I must call her that, not knowing her family name—as an obstruction.

"Beat it, Edith. I'll give you a buzz when they's somethin' doin'. Get on with that Blersdorf correspondence."

"O.K., boss," replied Edith, who made an exit with what I must feel was a provocative side-slip of her extremely flexible hips.

"There's a girl who knows her vegetables," remarked Mr. Smats admiringly as the door closed. "And you take Marybelle out at the telephone board. She's another. Why what that girl doesn't do to a

widower coming in here to buy his wife a funeral isn't worth thinking about. She hung a guy up for a thousand dollar spread only
yesterday, and he had come in talking about a hundred and fifty
dollar affair. But Edith is more subtle in a way. I use her after they
get by the gate."

As a matter of fact it had not struck me that there was anything
subtle about Edith. Mr. Smats smiled and shook his head reminiscently.

"And shape," he went on, "did you ever see a girl with more
shape than Edith? She's got just the least edge on Marybelle there."

I ventured once more to remind Mr. Smats that my time was
limited.

"Well," he said, tilting back in his swivel chair and at the same
time thrusting a box of cigars at me. "What's on your mind, Cornua? They haven't dug up any real evidence against you, have
they?"

"Mr. Killark has developed an interest in another aspect of the
case," I remarked, feeling my way.

"Yeah? He'll develop anything that will help earn him a pro-
motion. He developed some real estate over back of Flatbush once
that pretty nearly got him in Dutch with the League for Pure Politics. What did you say he is developing now?"

"A suspicion," I replied.

"Well, he always was a suspicious guy. You can't blame him for
suspecting something after a double murder and a hold-up. That's
what they pay him for."

"It's about you," I ventured.

Mr. Smats blew a smoke-ring toward the ceiling and watched
it dissipate.

"Say, Mr. Cornua—don't let that guy ride you. Why he's been
suspecting me—with and without cause—for the last ten years. Why
did he let me go after arresting me? Answer me that. I'll tell you—
you needn't speak. He knew damn well I could stand him on his
head if he pulled any phony stuff on me—that's why. Putting suspicions into your innocent head ain't goin' to get him anywhere.
Why doesn't he tell the papers Grierson killed Birmingham? Eh?

Because he's all fogged up over the shooting outside the house and doesn't know where he stands. If he talks or makes a move, all the papers will hand him a big laugh and a box of razzberries. Don't let that baby string you, Mr. Cornua."

"You know that Grierson killed Howard Birmingham?"

"Sure—just the way Killark knows it, but can't prove it. Why any moron who ever saw Times Square would know that much. Keeping the newspapers after you is just a grandstand play to kill time and hide his ignorance. Rule one,—when in doubt, charge the customer double. It's the old army game."

"When did you suspect Grierson?"

"That night—after I got a good look at you and the young lady. Of course, since you were paying me not to talk, I didn't say anything. Rule two—the customer is always right."

"Killark thinks you know something about the blackmail racket—is that what it's called?—at the Garden of Aphrodite."

"So that's it, eh? He lets the newspapers ride you to cover his own trail, and now he's going to climb out of his ignorance about the Grierson shooting by making me the hero of another fairy tale. All right—we'll see about that. By the time Killark gets through with me he won't know whether he's a detective or a salesman for birdseed. From now on, Mr. Cornua, you and me is allies. Forget the business side for the present—and when I get through and you and the young lady face Park Avenue again without a stain upon your characters, why then you can remember old Joe Smats, the square mortician."

"Thank you. I am certainly prepared to pay handsomely to be cleared of all suspicion—provided, of course, I am cleared by honorable means."

"Just leave the emphasis on the first part, Mr. Cornua. When I'm done I'll prove that man Killark has got parrot disease."

"Parrot disease?"

"Sure, talks out of turn and doesn't make sense."

"What steps will you take?"

"When I step out I make my own steps—I don't take 'em. I suppose you never heard of the Roslyn Club?"

"I can't say I have. My own is the University Club."

"Well, these lads didn't graduate from Harvard. The Roslyn Club is a bunch of hardworking boys off the sidewalks of New York. But what they don't know about what happens in this town is only the items in the Society column. Now I'm going to have 'em find me the answers to two questions. Who shot Grierson—and why—that's number one, and who worked the hundred fifty thou racket on baby doll—that's number two. When we get that news, we'll make your friend Killark look like the freckled side of a piece of tripe."

"But I thought that—er—well, that people in that station of life—er—er didn't betray each other?"

"Don't make me laugh, Cornua. I've got a new dental plate. The Roslyn boys don't like uncertainty, see?"

"I don't follow you."

"When a big racket has been pulled—such as this double murder and blackmail—it cramps everybody's style for a while. See?"

"No."

"Why, kick my hound, Mr. Cornua, all gangs is got to lay low until the right crowd is located, see? No one feels like taking a chance on calling attention to themselves while the breeze is blowin'. Nobody can't pull nothing, see? And to a bunch of nice boys in the liquor importing business, it's a handicap. Gets to be a question of 'when do we eat?'"

"I think I understand."

"Good for you. Now you run along and rest easy in your mind, Mr. Cornua. I suppose you've got a dick outside in the car watching you?"

"A what?"

"Detective. One of Killark's bright little boys."

"Mr. Killark mentioned that the chauffeur was on the force."

"Well, all he's got is an eyeful looking at Marybelle at the telephone desk. You hop out and say 'home, James' to him."

Mr. Smats rose and shook me heartily by the hand. I was uncertain, however, whether to feel relieved or anxious. To become a pawn in the warfare between Mr. Smats and Mr. Killark was enough

to give one pause. I stood outside the front door of Mr. Smats'
establishment and stared thoughtfully at my detective-chauffeur.

"What's next?" he asked at length.

"I think I'll look in on Miss Gorland on the way back to Mr.
Killark's office."

"Well, you'll have to make it snappy," the detective replied,
"because I'm supposed to deliver you before two."

"That will give me ample time," I replied, consulting my watch,
and noting at the same instant that the clock on the dashboard of
the car was three minutes and seven seconds fast. "To the house in
the east Eighties, if you please."

"You're the doctor," replied the detective incomprehensively.

# XI
## RIPPLES IN THE COURSE OF TRUE LOVE

I WAS FORTUNATE ENOUGH to find Julia at home, although not alone. In the first place there was the young man called Billy, who hailed from New Haven, and in the second place, Julia introduced me to a tall, elderly lady—a Miss Ponsonby-Stillwell—whom, I gathered, Julia had engaged as companion-chaperon, since otherwise she would be alone in the house with all the servants to look after.

Miss Ponsonby-Stillwell was garbed in densest black and seemed to regard the world pessimistically.

"Ever since my dear father passed on," remarked Miss Ponsonby-Stillwell, as I sat down, "I have seen nothing but trouble. First, the lawyers sold the estate, which hardly paid for poor pa-pa's debts, and then came my operations for which, of course, I had to have specialists and trained nurses, and now I find myself in this house with the black shadow of doom hanging over it."

"Don't you worry, Miss Ponsy," said Billy. "Mr. Cornua and I are going to put our heads together and pull Julia out of this business with flying colors. Just try looking on the bright side of things."

"When you have seen as much sorrow and suffering as I have, Mr. William, you will not be flippant in the presence of the grim reaper."

"Billy's name isn't William, dear Miss Hester," said Julia. "Just call him by his nickname 'Billy.' Neither he nor I can endure his real name—Sebastian. It sounds like something in Shakespeare."

"I read Shakespeare once," said Billy reminiscently, "in Freshman year. I always thought that old bird Lear was a nut for giving away his kingdom—but the prof said it was great tragedy. S'funny what things profs pick on. Father says it's because they're too theoretical—they haven't had a practical business training."

"I love *Romeo and Juliet*," Julia mused.

"Say, you said something," Billy cut in, eager to agree with his friend, "but why didn't he elope with her? That's what beats me. 'Course, I know it's poetry and all that—and you can't expect poetry to have too much sense, except in the hidden meanings which the prof digs out—but it would have been a cinch to give that story a happy ending—like real life."

"I think," I interrupted, although loath to cut short Billy's theories of literary criticism, "that Julia and I have several important matters to discuss. Further, as far as present time is concerned, I am not entirely a free agent."

"Is there any news, Cousin Robert?" Julia asked. "Are they still keeping you in prison?"

"Perhaps—if I should withdraw?" and Miss Ponsonby-Stillwell arose.

"I regret the necessity—but if you would be so kind?" I agreed. I felt the reply to Julia's question about my being in prison was too technical for general broadcasting.

Miss Ponsonby-Stillwell sighed heavily and left the room.

"As for me, I shall stick 'round," announced Billy. "Three heads are better than two."

"I have no objection," I conceded, "since you may be able to assist Julia. First, Mr. Killark, the detective, and Mr. Smats have independently come to the conclusion, Julia, that Grierson killed your uncle."

"Good work!" cried Billy, "I mean" (suddenly abashed) "that it lifts suspicion off you, Uncle Robert."

"Uncle Robert?" I said severely.

I saw Julia blush.

"Well, that's maybe a little premature, but I had to call you something and Mr. Cornua sounds foolish," Billy apologized.

"I shall permit Uncle Robert for the present," I announced.

The young man's charm was disarming, and I preferred not to raise the question of my family name.

"But why should our butler want to kill Uncle Howard?" asked Julia, the tears coming to her eyes once more.

The poor child had made a desperate struggle ever since the fatal evening to live up to her modern code of not showing emotion publicly—to continue to appear light-hearted and inconsequential—and the strain was getting to be too much for her stoicism to endure, since in fact she had loved her uncle like a father.

"That we don't yet know," I answered, "nor why Grierson was himself shot down."

"Let's make a theory," suggested Billy.

"Oh, do, Uncle Robert. We must find the murderer. Think of a theory."

"Mr. Killark is trying to think of one now, my dear."

"I know," said Julia, "but he's only a policeman, not a philosopher and college man like you. You ought to be able to think of heaps of better theories, Bobbie. Try!"

Whenever Julia teases me for anything I cease for the moment being Cousin Robert and become Bobbie to her.

"Mr. Smats has a better scheme than the invention of a theory, my dear. He is going to have the Roslyn Club find out for us."

"I never heard of that crowd. Who are they?" asked Billy.

"They are, I infer, an underworld gang with access to rather exclusive information, if they choose to seek it."

"Do you suppose I could get put up for that club?" Billy cut in eagerly. "I'd like to help, you know—do something active, not just sit around helpless like I've been doing."

"Billy, you couldn't join an underworld gang."

"For you I would," said Billy simply, but with meaning.

Julia flushed a delicate and very beautiful pink, and I sighed a little inwardly when I saw the light in her eyes as she looked at Billy.

"Youth—youth," I thought once more, "how I envy you." Luckily the young people were blissfully unaware that I was capable of any feeling. I must not mar their dawning happiness with the least shadow of a regret, I reflected.

"You know, Billy," I said, "I'll give your suggestion to Mr. Smats. Perhaps he can use you."

"Gee, that would be swell!"

"Billy, I won't hear of it!" cried Julia. "It's ridiculous."

"I don't see anything ridiculous," said Billy, expanding his one hundred and eighty-five pounds of football muscle. "It's certainly lousy just to sit and do nothing when you and Uncle Robert are caught in a jam."

His tone revealed hurt feelings.

"Billy, are you going to listen to me?"

I smiled to myself at the note of exasperation in Julia's voice, wondering how this first and probably determining contest for supremacy between these two children would come out.

"Now, honey, I just can't when it's a question of your safety," replied Billy, with a pleasant firmness which gave me great satisfaction. Julia would find a master, but one who would also know when to be indulgent.

"Then I won't speak to you again, Sebastian," said Julia rising.

I knew she intended the use of Billy's true name Sebastian as the crowning symbol of permanent rupture. But what high-spirited colt was ever tamed on the first morning?

"Very well, *Miss* Gorland," said Billy, also rising. "Uncle Robert," he remarked, turning to me, "will you let me have the address of Mr. Smats' office, please?"

"Certainly," I answered, gnawing my lip to keep from smiling at the indignant tragedy registered in the faces of the two young persons.

"I must ask you not to call Mr. Cornua 'Uncle Robert'—it is not showing him proper respect," Julia spoke, with words that felt like the draft from a Frigidaire.

It occurred to me that she had let "Uncle Robert" pass a moment before. I handed Billy a card on which I scribbled the address of Mr. Smats' mortuary parlors in the Bronx.

"And don't let the two-headed blonde get you," I said. "Buy no funeral without consulting me first."

"What on earth are you talking about, Bobbie?" asked Julia, feminine curiosity overcoming female indignation, as I had planned my remark to effect.

"The portal of Mr. Smats' underworld," I replied, "is guarded not by a three-headed Cerberus, like the famous underworld of antiquity, but, as I said before, by a two-headed blonde."

"Do you really mean a freak—but there aren't such things," protested Julia, logic adding a spur to her curiosity.

Billy was not paying any attention, for he was absorbed in his hurt feelings, which he relieved by slowly revolving his felt hat.

"You mean tow-headed," Julia added.

"No, I don't. I mean two-headed. If the one at the telephone booth allows you to escape without signing for something handsome, then her counterpart, alike but more subtle spiritually I am informed, waylays you in the cave of the winds and from thence there is no returning save by writing your spell upon the dotted line."

"You mean Mr. Smats has two blonde secretaries?"

"You have penetrated to the essence of my figurative language," I replied.

"I wonder why men always hire blonde stenographers? It's that book Anita Loos wrote, I suppose. Everybody knows that blondes are dumb," Julia pouted.

"Not these," I said in rebuttal. "They may be exceptions to your rule—I shall concede you that much—but these are not only as wise as the serpent, but sway with somewhat of the same lissome grace when in movement."

"Billy isn't likely to fall for persons of that type," said Julia, off her guard.

"Then you aren't sore—" Billy cut in, his voice vibrant with hope.

A football coach, I reflected, would have rebuked him for picking an opening so clumsily. After all I had done by way of interference for him in taking out the secondary defence of Julia's anger, he had to go and give his play away like that. Of course, Julia did not miss her tackle.

"If you go to that address," said Julia, indicating the card I had given Billy, "I won't speak to you again—that's flat. Besides, I can't see that Cousin Robert's and my affairs are any of your business anyway. It's too important a matter for a mere boy without any experience to butt into."

I was tempted to murmur "Thrown for a loss of thirty-five yards," but refrained on grounds of public and private policy.

"Well, gee whiz!" sputtered Billy, chained helplessly within his emotions by a vocabulary inadequate for their outlet. "I—I—I'll just show you—and Uncle Rob—I mean Mr. Cornua—that I'm not such a bonehead as—as you think me. I'll make you sorry Julia Gorland," he added, with a feebly desperate attempt to be tragic or melodramatic, "good-bye!" and he stalked out of the house.

"Oh, Bobbie! Will he be in any danger? Can't you stop him?" said the by now illogical Julia.

For a moment I envied those old men of medieval story who were always smiling in their beards. At forty-five, when one is clean-shaven in order not to look fifty, it is extremely difficult to veil a smile.

"I have an idea," I said soothingly, "that that boy has the stuff in him to pull himself out of any scrape and what is even better— to pull someone he likes out too."

By way of answer Julia laid her head on my shoulder and sobbed. I was extremely disconcerted for, as I have explained before, tears were contrary to Julia's private code of conduct. Often had I heard her discourse of the silliness of the Victorian girl who was not only always weeping but also had to have a masculine shoulder for a foundation. She had thanked heaven with much fervor that the modern generation was not like that. I determined at this moment somewhat to revise the theme-idea of my book of philosophy and to predicate it on the assumption that fundamentally human nature does not change.

And that thought brought me to another. I wished, as Julia kept her face snugly hidden on my shoulder, that I could change my own human nature. Since the night of Howard Birmingham's murder I had become aware of a new and disturbing fact, namely that I, Robert Cornua, middle-aged philosopher and dilettante, who had never before looked at or thought about women seriously, was now in love with my young and beautiful god-child. What a tragedy for me at my time of life! What refuge, what solace can there be for a hopeless love?—for hopeless it had to be. Had I not been witness to the true-lover's quarrel between Julia and Billy? No hint of my own selfish feeling should be allowed to cloud that natural and inevitable call of youth to youth. To coax Julia away from Billy, supposing such a thing were even possible, would be to ruin Julia's future happiness. I should die in the fullness of time, leaving her behind a young widow but past the first flush of her beauty—and then the empty years without a husband would stare her in the face, occupied only with the emptiness that money can buy—Paris, the Riviera, Palm Beach, Bar Harbor—what not—a barren Odyssey with no Ithaca at the end—no Hesperides left to sail to.

Better a thousand times to relinquish her to Billy and to the touzled heads that in future would play about these two—and perhaps one of them—I smiled in spite of myself at the thought—would go to Yale and in the words of the old college song "lick the Harvards, like his daddy used to do." All of which proves only that a middle-aged philosopher is a hopeless sentimentalist. I suspect that most of us become Victorian at forty-five—openly so, I mean.

And it was Julia herself who gave me the *coup-de-grâce*. She looked up, brushed away her lustrous tears, kissed me and said: "I love you, Bobbie. You are the only daddy I've got now—the only one in the world I can turn to."

"Yes, dear," I whispered, rather proud that my words did not tremble. "I shall always be your dad now, no matter what happens," and I kissed her again.

"Daddy Bob," she went on, suddenly christening me anew—I quivered a little at the inevitableness—"You—you like Billy, don't you?"

She was examining minutely the lapel of my lounge jacket. Her copper hair just brushed its glories lightly against my chin.

"Yes, dear child—if you do."

"I—I think I do—I'm almost sure. He—he hasn't said anything—I wouldn't let him—but—but—"

"I know. And what of his family and all that, dear?"

"They are all right, Bobby dad—not that that matters as long— as long as Billy's all right—and he is, Bobbie—in spite of this morning—when he was just being stubborn to show off—and I don't want him to get into danger and trouble on our account—he ought to go back to New Haven and finish his course."

"We'll send him back, I promise you, dear. Meanwhile I fancy he can take a week's vacation without too many obstacles accruing at the Dean's office. At least he will have an unusual excuse and that, in my college days, was a potent argument. Even deans appreciate novelty. Just now, for a day or two, dear, he can run errands for me to Joe Smats, if the district attorney decides to detain me. But I'll see he gets into no danger with the two blondes or from any other source."

"I wasn't thinking of that," said Julia with dignity. "Billy isn't that kind. It's the gunmen—and things like that."

"I don't think Mr. Smats will let him do anything dangerous. Mr. Smats has a truly professional distrust of amateurs. And Billy couldn't be happy if he didn't think he is doing something to help."

"I know," said Julia and wiped her eyes with the usual scrap of lace.

Involuntarily I glanced at my watch and started. It was nineteen minutes after one and I must have come near to exhausting the patience of my detective-chauffeur.

"I shall come back again just as soon as I can," I said reassuringly.

Julia clung tightly to me once more, and then I left with no more word spoken.

Thirty-seven minutes later I reported at the district attorney's office.

# XII
## LUNCHEON AT BOUDELON'S

Upon my arrival at the district-attorney's office I was cross-questioned once more by this sharp-spoken official and his aide, Mr. Killark of the Homicide Squad. The interview was necessarily painful to me for although these gentlemen did not appear to doubt my innocence, they were still in the awkward predicament of not being able to prove either to the newspapers or to the public that I had no criminal connection with Howard Birmingham's murder. The circumstantial evidence against me would remain overwhelming until Mr. Killark or Mr. Smats could find the missing factors. The district attorney was compelled, therefore, to continue a nominal detention of me as a material witness, but arranged at the same time to make matters as comfortable as he could. I had liberty to move about provided only that I was always accompanied by a detective.

Mr. Killark lingered a moment in my assigned quarters after the district attorney left. He summarized my position as follows: "You see, Cornua, there's hardly a job pulled off that we don't know who done it, but the hell of it is to get proof that will impress a jury—to say nothing of getting by on cross-examination. Now, here's what I'm up against. We haven't got the blackmailer yet— and so we haven't got the gang that shot Grierson. 'Course, any day now we may round the whole crowd up, and then you'll be sittin' pretty—because it'll be easy enough to establish connections. You can thank your lucky stars, Mr. Cornua, that those guys made the misplay of shootin' Grierson. That one error is going to cost them the ball game. If they'd let him make his get-away, there'd been nothin' left but the circumstantial evidence against you—or against the girl, Miss Julia. But you see, they tied themselves up with what happened inside by killing the butler—and that will let you out in time. It's a cinch you didn't pay the blackmail as a blind— see? We can show that all right. I know the newspapers have got you sittin' on a tack just now—but when we get all through, think of the fine publicity it will be for that book you're writing."

"I confess," I remarked, "that that consolation had not crossed my mind."

"Sure—why say—you wouldn't have a Chinaman's chance of cashing in on a book about philosophy just by yourself. That stuff's too damn highbrow to go over big. But you could rebind last year's telephone directories and sell 'em now as 'Cornua's Inside Story.' Gee, I'll say it's a lucky break for you."

"Possibly we differ in our definition of good fortune," I said mildly.

"I know you're sore just now—and I don't blame you, with all your friends and the newspapers saying worse things about you than if you was a Bolshevik, but you'll have the laugh on 'em yet— and the satisfaction of crossin' a few names off your visiting list. Christmas will be cheaper for you next year, don't forget that."

With these final words of good cheer, Mr. Killark revolved his cigar and arose.

"There's just one word for your friend," he said at the door. "You tell Joe Smats that he can't get away with a thing. As long as he shows bonafides and helps you, I'll lay off him—but any funny business and he'll be toastmaster at the next banquet of the Roslyn Club in the Tombs. On the other hand—and this you can tell him is straight dope—good information will help cross off some of the red in the ledger. But he's got to watch his step," and Mr. Killark closed the door behind him softly.

Almost instantly the door reopened part way and I saw Mr. Killark's cigar slowly protrude through the crack.

"One thing more, Mr. Cornua," came the voice from behind the cigar, "when we've got this little business of ours settled, will you please tell me the true story about you and Joe Smats? I'll give you guarantees not to use it—but my curiosity just can't stand the strain."

Mr. Killark's eyes followed the cigar into the room.

"You always refuse to believe it when I tell you," I replied.

He sighed deeply, which act blew a little cloud of smoke toward the ceiling.

"You'll trust me some day," he remarked enigmatically, and closed the door again.

It appeared impossible to rid this man's mind of the peculiar obsession that in some way or other Joe Smats and I had been allies in other business transactions. The implication was not, of course, complimentary to me, but then it was less defamatory than the current articles about me in the newspapers. Further, when all was said and done, I reflected, I had justified even the worst suspicions. The more I thought my position over, the greater fool I appeared to have been—and yet, I concluded, I would do it all over again today if the need to help Julia arose. Had I not stepped into the house in the East Eighties on that fatal night, the same suspicions would inevitably have made Julia their victim. Not, of course, that I got to thinking of myself as a hero or a martyr to self-sacrifice or any rot like that—one does the natural thing inevitably, that's all—and there was no one left of her stock to do it for Julia but me. The clan rallies when the fiery cross appears. No more than that.

Two days after my last talk with Mr. Killark, time which I had spent in my detention quarters under special orders from the district attorney, there came an alteration in my position. For some reason not revealed to me, the authorities hinted at sensational new developments in the Birmingham murder. Mr. Killark, I heard, had gone to Chicago, hence I was not able to learn the details, for the district attorney also sent word that he was too busy to see me. But what was far better, I was released from detention and from the necessity of having a detective-chauffeur conduct me wherever I went. I was free to send for Martin and the Packard, a privilege which I immediately accepted.

I told Martin when he came to drive me uptown to my apartment on Park Avenue. Forty-eight hours since I had seen Julia—what on earth should I do when she had her own apartment with Billy and an old codger would no longer have any excuse for too frequent visits? But another thought struck me while we were waiting for a traffic light to turn green—past, present, and future would jumble themselves in my head—why had I been released without any explanation? The answer occurred to me while Martin was dodging a wild taxi in Union Square. It was that old suspicion of Killark's concerning my relations with Joe Smats. I was to be turned loose and of course watched to see what would happen. Mr. Killark probably expected that I would in some way reveal the exact connection, if I believed myself free of all suspicion. Had the matter not been so serious, it would have pleased me immensely to lead Mr. Killark on a wild-goose chase, but under the circumstances I resolved to be circumspect. My interviews with Mr. Smats would be strictly limited to getting from him his promised information.

At twelve-fourteen we arrived at my apartment and I requested Evans to telephone Miss Julia and ask her if she would do me the honor to lunch with me at Boudelon's. I felt the need of some *hors d'oeuvres* and a crisp roll with fresh butter. Eating under detention, as I had been doing for the past two days, jades one's appetite. In a moment the reply came through, via Evans, that she would be delighted, if I had no objection to Billy's coming along. Evans relayed the message through the curtains of my shower-bath. I accepted the condition and told Evans to say one-twenty-one at the house in the East Eighties.

I stepped forth much refreshed from my shower and pleased to learn that Billy had been restored to Julia's good graces. It will be recalled that three days ago Billy had been cashiered for failure to obey orders. Evans had laid out exactly the right things for me to wear—a dignified gray with just a touch of color in cravat and handkerchief to symbolize my new freedom. He had selected, I noted, the star-sapphire cuff links.

I smoothed my hair—getting a bit thin on top, alas—and glanced at the manuscript of my book lying on the desk. An unfinished sentence stared at me, mute witness of Julia's interruption on the fatal night. I read: "In the scheme of the Cosmos, one fact is evident, namely, that—" and the sentence broke off. To this day, although the book has been finished and published, I do not recall what the one fact is that was evident in the scheme of the Cosmos.

There was a huge heap of correspondence unopened beside the manuscript—mostly abuse I guessed from my experience of the few letters I had read since Howard's murder.

"Have Miss Serad run through these," I said to Evans—referring to my secretary—"and make notes of anything I should know. If there are any bills, she may pay them—but I am not to be bothered, tell her."

"Quite," said Evans.

"And remember, Evans, I have no engagements until further orders. It's no good Miss Serad writing things on my engagement pad. I shan't look at it."

"I understand, sir."

"I may dine tonight—oh, I've already told you to have dinner every night."

"It was a delicious wild duck last night, sir," said Evans. "It was a pity you missed that, if you'll pardon the liberty."

"I am glad you enjoyed it, Evans."

"With wild rice," he added reminiscently.

"Quite a wild party," I ventured with a joke which I hoped would be within the range of Evans' intellect.

"I beg your pardon, sir—the chef and I were quite alone," he said, drawing himself up, with offended dignity. "I am not in the 'abit, sir—"

"Wild duck—wild rice—wild party—see, Evans?" I cut in.

He thought for a moment and then coughed behind his hand.

"Quite so, sir. Very good—very good, indeed. A facetious play upon words, sir. I beg your pardon."

"Have something tame tonight, Evans."

"Very good, sir. Saddle of spring lamb?"

"That will do nicely," and I left him closing the door softly after me.

I found Billy and Julia waiting for me—I arrived at the exact instant I had set—in a state of wild excitement. Billy, it turned out, when I had sifted the interruptions of these two young people who both tried to tell me at once, had seen the head waiter of the Garden of Aphrodite—the man to whom I had handed the package contained one hundred and fifty thousand dollars—in the subway crowd at the 96th Street station. He stepped from a Broadway local just as Billy's Bronx express pulled out of the station. Billy realized it was useless to take the next train back, so he did a better thing, went on to Joe Smats' as he had intended, and reported his discovery there.

"Billy simply had to come and tell me next," explained Julia, "and that is how I came to forgive him."

She seemed to regard this explanation as entirely logical.

"It proves, at least," I commented, "that one member of the blackmail gang is still in town."

"A darned good deduction," said Billy. "I made the same one."

"What did Smats say?"

"Well, Smats—he's a good scout at that— thought what we do, only he knows all about that headwaiter and says he's never been in a racket before until this one, so he doesn't yet know the gang he's tied up with—but being in town makes finding out pretty soft."

"If he got off a Broadway local at 96ᵗʰ Street, he must have got on at a station above 72nd Street," I mused.

"Bobbie, you're wonderful!" Julia cried. "I'd never have thought of that!"

"He must have come from somewhere and been going somewhere—the question is where and which?" I continued with my train of reasoning. "What are the streets nearest to 79th, which is the first local station above 72nd?"

"Why, 78th and 80th," said Julia triumphantly.

"I was thinking rather of what places—night-clubs and speakeasies—might be in that neighborhood."

"You said streets," objected Julia.

"I asked Joe Smats what he thought about that," said Billy. "Joe answered that he never wasted time thinking when it was easy to find out. That's swell dope. I'll try that line on some prof. when I get back to New Haven."

"Now, Billy, don't you run any risk of flunking out of college," Julia reproved him.

"Shall we talk this over at luncheon?" I suggested.

"I'm hungry as a bear. Let's!" and Julia jumped up. "Bobbie, I want some artichokes with Hollandaise, mushrooms *sous clôche* and a *café parfait*. You can add the rest when we get there."

"I believe I feel like a steak," remarked Billy, whose taste in food was always reminiscent of the training table.

"The mushrooms before the artichokes, please," she whispered, as we climbed into my car.

Boudelon's is a pleasant place, not perhaps as "ritzy"—to borrow one of Julia's adjectives—as some others, but the cooking and service are genuinely French and not delicatessen disguised as Savarin. One can even play dominoes, only one doesn't.

"Don't forget, sir," said Billy apologetically while the waiter threatened me with pad and pencil from behind my chair, "that the French idea of a steak is a piece of meat with a very limited area. Even the double sirloin—well, I'll leave it to you, Uncle Robert. Julia said you were known in Paris as a regular gourmand."

"Gourmet, Billy!" exclaimed Julia indignantly.

"I never was very hot at French," apologized Billy.

A profusion of *hors d'oeuvres variés* arrived. Julia squealed with delight as she picked and chose. Billy, I observed, took everything of which hardboiled eggs were the foundation. And then came Billy's steak, which the waiter not unnaturally supposed was for the three of us, and indeed might well have served a group at a neighboring table as well. Billy fell upon it with knife and fork not greedily, as might be thought, but with the normal enthusiastic appetite of his size and age. Julia toyed daintily with her mushrooms and I with my omelette *bonne femme*. When I believed that the silence and Billy's steak might well end together, I spoke again, reminding the two youngsters that the object of our assembly was to discuss our problem.

"Joe Smats didn't think much of putting me up for the Roslyn Club—it's kind of an exclusive crowd. You have to have a sort of high standing in the bootlegging business before they will even consider you—he said—and come from one of the well-known families over on Avenue A," Billy began.

"Billy," said Julia, "Mr. Smats showed more sense than you did."

"Well, I still think," said Billy, "if they could meet me and find out I'm a regular guy, they might let me in. As for that headwaiter at the Garden of Aphrodite, Joe did think that important. That he would risk going around in New York and be recognized, Smats considered showed two things—either a new racket was about ready to break, or the police were on a totally wrong scent and the crowd thought it safe to crawl out of their holes."

"A new racket? What's that?" asked Julia.

"Some more funny business—like the holdup of you and Uncle Robert—and the other thing."

Billy meant to be tactful in referring to Howard Birmingham's murder as "the other thing."

"I think it more likely," I said to reassure Julia, whose eyes filled again at the thought of her Uncle Howard, "that they believe the police are convinced of my guilt and therefore the coast is clear again."

"I don't believe they're such boobs as that," commented Billy.

"What is Mr. Smats going to do next?" I asked.

"He's waiting for a report from the executive committee of the Roslyn Club—anyway the main guys in the crowd—about the headwaiter tonight. He suggested you and I drop up to his office some time."

"At what time, Billy?"

"I didn't ask—after dinner, I guess. Say nine o'clock."

"Why should I say nine o'clock if you don't know when we are expected?"

"Well, nine o'clock sounds reasonable."

"Julia," I said, "in your leisure moments I hope you will instruct this young man in the meaning and value of time. At present any hour of the day or night seems utterly immaterial to him."

"I'll try, Cousin Robert."

I went out of the room to a telephone booth and was informed by the voice of Mr. Smats' secretary—the one at the front door, I believe—that he would be pleased to see me at the time I set, namely nine forty-five. I did not care to hurry Evans over dinner and it was a long way from my apartment to Mr. Smats' establishment.

When I returned Julia made an unexpected announcement.

"Cousin Robert," she said, "I am going with you and Billy tonight. I just can't face an evening alone with my chaperon, Miss Ponsonby-Stillwell, listening to her accounts of her operations."

"But, my dear child—" I began by way of protest.

"Why, is there any danger? Because if there is, you and Billy aren't going either."

"No danger, of course—just a consultation with Mr. Smats."

"Then there's no reason why I shouldn't go. I can sit outside in the car and wait while you two listen to Mr. Smats."

There was some more argument, but as usual with Julia when she made up her mind, there could be only one outcome—an agreement to accept her decision. I paid the check with some misgivings—it was really extraordinary what Boudelon's charged for Billy's steak—but my misgivings were not caused by the amount of the check. I had a feeling that Julia should not go with us. There was no help for it, however; she was resolved, therefore I asked her and Billy to dine with me at my apartment at seven-thirty. Probably we can stretch the saddle of lamb, I thought, although the recollection of Billy's steak was not reassuring on this point.

"And please remind Billy," I said, as I parted from the youngsters after luncheon, "that dinner at seven-thirty means exactly that."

"I'm never late to meals," said Billy.

Knowing what I now knew of him, I am inclined to think he spoke the truth.

# XIII
## MR. SMATS LOSES THE FIRST BATTLE

WHEN WE REACHED Mr. Smat's consolatory emporium with its potted palms in gigantic Chinese vases, now illuminated by a subdued indirect lighting system, we found blonde number one, Marybelle, on faithful guard by the outer switchboard. Julia elected to remain in my limousine under the protection of my chauffeur Martin, although her curiosity led her to steal one look at Marybelle through the plate glass door. I judged from the expression on Julia's face that her preconceived opinion of Mr. Smats' aide had been confirmed, if wrinkling up a very dainty nose means anything.

Marybelle smiled graciously at me and extended a long, tapering hand manicured to the last possible degree of white and pink perfection, which I shook a little unconvincingly in my surprise at her condescension. Billy, I observed, she ignored with deliberate hauteur.

"Mr. Smats will see you immediately," she said in the flute-like tones cultivated by private switchboard operators. "Walk right in, Mr. Cornua."

We opened the oaken gate carved richly in Gothic style, and leaving Marybelle's extremely obvious knees behind us, strode down the solemn corridor to Mr. Smats' office. There the more subtle lady, as Mr. Smats had described her, Edith, received us, or rather me, for she too affected to be unaware of Billy's presence, and another hand of rare finish was laid in my palm for a fleeting instant. Mr. Smats rose from his desk and came cordially forward.

132

"Have one of the boys drive you and Marybelle home, Edith," he said, "I won't want you girls again tonight. Hullo, Cornua—how's the suspect?"

"All righty, Mr. Smats," replied Edith to her dismissal, with a more bell-like than fluty note, and she left us alone.

"Good evening," I said as Mr. Smats shook my hand with great enthusiasm. "We have called hoping for news."

"There's plenty—nothing else but," said Mr. Smats, thrusting Billy and me into chairs. "Right on time, I see," he said consulting a watch which did not appear to me to be a reliable type.

Billy lit a cigarette while Mr. Smats passed his cigar humidor— one so large that it reminded me forcibly of those other chests it was partly Mr. Smats' business to sell. I noted that silence was becoming a strain on Billy.

"The news?" I suggested, for Mr. Smats appeared to have passed into a day-dream behind a cloud of tobacco smoke.

"The Roslyn boys have submitted a report," he chuckled. "Old Killark would give five years of his pension to hear it. While he's tootin' around in Chicago lookin' for the business end of a rainbow, the big news breaks right here."

"Yes?" I urged, as Mr. Smats again relapsed into puffing smoke rings. "Will you communicate with the police?"

"Will I communicate with Silas G. Lucifer?" said Mr. Smats scornfully, and hit a high brass utensil with emphatic accuracy. "We play this hand out with our own cards, Cornua. You offered a reward of $50,000, I believe?"

"Certainly."

"O. K. I don't feel like making Sam Killark a present of any part of it—he can stick to his real estate business."

"But what in heaven's name, Mr. Smats, have you found out?" I asked impatiently.

"Keep calm, Cornua. This is too good to spill just like a winner at Acqueduct. First, will you see me protected on the reward? No cutting up with a bunch of cops who will come rushin' in after I've done their job for 'em?"

"I guarantee for the full amount of the reward, if your information is what we need."

"Fair enough. I've just had Edith type out a little paper here to that effect. You gotta be business-like in this world, Cornua."

"Certainly," I agreed, reading through and signing the document he handed me.

"'Course," said Mr. Smats, scrutinizing my signature, "I'd be willing to trust you, Cornua, in a gentleman's agreement, but you see me and Killark ain't gentlemen—not in that sense of the word, we ain't—so I prefer black and white, both in bottle and on paper. Billy, if you know how to write, just add your John Hancock as a witness."

I admired Billy for swallowing the insult without a word. He scrawled his name with a jade green fountain pen almost the size of a baseball bat.

"See-bastian?" said Mr. Smats over Billy's shoulder.

"That is my Christian name," said Billy haughtily.

"Well, I'll be—." Mr. Smats did not finish the sentence. "I wonder if it's legal with a name like that on it? Who'd believe it?"

"Nevertheless, that is my legal name," said Billy. "If you don't like it, you know what you can do about it."

"Billy!" I interrupted warningly.

"Don't get ratty, kid," said Mr. Smats with a grin. "I don't have much fun in my business. You gotta make allowances. See-bastian—well, of all the—."

"How about the information, now the legal matter is settled?" asked Billy, compressing his lips.

"I'll just file this myself," said Mr. Smats, folding up the paper and putting it away in his wallet. "I don't think it's decent to let Edith see a name like that. Now we'll talk turkey."

"Yes," I encouraged him.

"The Roslyn boys started with Billy's tip here that the head-waiter from the Garden of Aphrodite was still in town—and they put some more crowds wise, because business has been pretty bad with this thing stirrin' up the newspapers. We picked that guy up along about five o'clock, crowded him into a taxi, and he's thinkin' things over in a cellar under a garage. They got him pretty scared, because you see he ain't a regular racketeer—or we'd known things earlier. He claims he just acted as go-between, for a cash consideration, to receive a packet of money from you, Cornua. The blackmail gang had to have a guy not too well-known to police and us professionals, see? 'Course, this lad had been doin' stuff over the radio, but he wasn't one of us, and had no connections to put us wise. Well, he doesn't like that cellar where he's stopping now— there's no hot and cold water and no radio in it—and he doesn't like the racket because he got gypped out of his price—and his only company is a bunch of boys kinda anxious to make him talk—so after some persuasion from a piece of hose—he did."

Mr. Smats paused and shut his eyes reflectively.

"Do you mean you tortured him?" I asked horrified.

"We only hurt his feelings, as it turned out, Cornua. When he got a good look at the guy with the piece of hose, we didn't have to use it. I never believe in bein' cruel, Cornua, when kindness will do the trick. Don't push me, and I'll never hurt a fly."

"I cannot allow violence—or illegal methods," I said.

"Violence is always bad business—and I don't use it," affirmed Mr. Smats. "Illegal methods is more a matter of opinion, but I ain't goin' to argue now. We found out the guy he turned the packet over to, though—because the headwaiter was ignorant of my principles and the piece of hose looked convincing. The blackmailer is Ed Flippenhauser, international confidence man and high-grade Society flimflammer. He answers the description Miss Julia gave of the fellow she knew as Dudley Flurrel. Well, that ain't all. Along about half past six we dug Ed out of a joint over in Hoboken—and we've got him up in a loft over the East River where we can get him away handy enough by motor speedboat if they's need for a quick jump."

"Do you mean to say that you are acting as if you were police and holding these two men prisoners?"

"I'm acting better than the police—they've been a week on this job and have only got hold of you. Now I've got the really important answer while Killark is driving around Chicago like a Chautauqua lecturer."

"But—but—it's illegal—you will get us all in worse trouble than ever, Mr. Smats."

"Say, Cornua, you're a good one to talk about illegal methods after that little party you let me in for. What I'm doing is an Epworth League picnic compared to the stunt you tried to pull off with Birmingham's body. Besides, Killark will be pretty grateful for everything when the show-down comes, except for losing out on the reward. That's goin' to gripe him—but I'll fix that by lettin' him have the credit for the arrests. What they used to tell me in Sunday school—virtue is its own reward."

It was difficult for me to visualize Mr. Smats in Sunday school.

"And the next move?" inquired Billy.

"The next move—See-bastian," replied Mr. Smats with humorous emphasis upon Billy's unfortunate name, "is more or less up to Killark. At this stage of the game Ed isn't going to do much talking, especially as the blackmail business is the only open and shut case against him. The murders is somethin' else again and for the present, I'm goin' to leave 'em lay. I heard today Killark is flyin' back by plane from Chicago. He's run out of clues again."

"I should like to know how you found these two criminals so quickly," I said.

"Don't let that worry you, Cornua. It's a long story and you'd not be any wiser if I told you. The Roslyn boys are good—that's all you need to hear."

"I always thought that—er—er—well, that there is a code or something—to—er—prevent—er—telling on each other," I ventured as tactfully as I could.

"You mean that old bunk about honor—don't kid yourself, Cornua. Fifty thousand dollars is a chunk of real money—and besides, everyone is tired of waitin' for this to blow over. It is only business to get it out of the way."

"Thank you for your assistance, Mr. Smats," I said rising, "I don't know what I should have done without you."

"I know," he replied. "You'd probably have gone to the electric chair on circumstantial evidence—that's what you would have done. You can think that over any time you want to feel grateful. I'll send for you in the morning when Killark gets back."

He shook hands with me at this and clapped Billy heartily on the back, to that young man's discomfiture.

"If you need champagne for the wedding, See-bastian," he said, "I can lay my hands on a few cases of the real stuff—and the price will be right, seein's it's you."

Mr. Smats followed us down the corridor. Billy and I passed through the plate glass revolving door and stepped into the street. My car was not in sight, nor, when I looked up and down the street, could I see it parked anywhere. A horrible sinking sensation seized me. Billy shouted. Mr. Smats heard him and hastily joined us in the street.

"The car—Julia—has gone," cried Billy.

"Maybe she got tired waitin' and went home. She'll send it back for you."

"Telephone—quick—and see, will you?" I said, my alarm growing.

I knew Julia would not go home without letting us know. She was capricious but too thoughtful of others to do a thing like that. Mr. Smats stepped in to his telephone board. In a moment he came back, shaking his head.

"She's not at her house, or at your apartment, Cornua. Of course, she may not have arrived yet—still, I don't quite like it. I guess I'll 'phone a couple of the Roslyn boys," and he went back.

Billy and I stared at each other in silence under the electric street lights. Our faces were expressive enough without words. Inside we could see Mr. Smats seated with the headpiece of Marybelle's telephone over his ears. He was talking rapidly. We went in and stood beside him. He pulled out a plug and slipped off the headgear.

"They'll be right along—a couple of good boys. Now you and See-bastian keep your shirts on. No harm will come to the young lady—just remember that. It's a trade, see? We let Ed go and they'll let her go—"

"Then you think she's been kidnapped?"

"I don't think—I know. I was a damn fool to send Marybelle home—if she had been watching from her place by the door, it couldn't have happened. I guess I'm gettin' overconfident in my old age."

"But I can't understand Martin—he had positive orders from me to wait."

"Oh, it's easy enough to think up a plausible message."

"Thank heaven Killark will be here tomorrow!"

"So you think Killark can settle this, eh? All right. I'll call the Roslyn boys off," and Mr. Smats picked up his telephone.

"Stop!" I called out, while Billy seized Mr. Smats' arm.

"Easy, gents, easy," said that imperturbable person. "I got a slight touch of rheumatiz in my left elbow. What's the play, gents—put your money anywhere you wish, it's all one to me, red or black, odd or even."

"Fifty thousand dollars cash for Miss Julia safe and sound!" I shouted.

"Now you're saying words, Mr. Cornua. That's a language I understand. But I'm no Shylock. I'll get the girl back—without any promises—only I won't have Killark in on it, see? This is a private matter now between the Roslyns and Ed Flippenhauser's gang. We'll have to settle it in our own way. Nobody is going to come up to my front door and get away with stuff like that. I know an insult when I get one."

"But Killark will be back in the morning and find Julia gone."

"He'll find more than that. He'll find us all gone. You and Seebastian here are coming with me and the Roslyn boys—and we'll leave no address behind."

"But—but—" I protested.

"You want to get Miss Julia safe—and quick?"

"Yes—yes—for God's sake, yes!" cried Billy.

"Then you gotta trust Joe Smats, the square mortician. Is it a go?"

"Yes," I said.

There was a look in Joe Smats' eyes I had never seen there before, a look that gave me confidence he was in earnest. Besides, had he not found the blackmailer within a few hours of receiving the first tip, while Killark was still beating the bush in vain? So, when Mr. Smats extended his hand, I shook it warmly in token of my faith.

# XIV
## MR. SMATS' LAIR

WITHIN THIRTEEN MINUTES during which time Mr. Smats had been doing some telephoning, he ushered us into a closed car on the front seat of which sat, next to the chauffeur, a shadowy figure whom my host briefly identified as "one of the Roslyn boys"—or, in other words, I suppose a body-guard. Billy sat hunched in one corner as the car moved off rapidly with us.

"Where to?" Billy asked Mr. Smats.

"Where it will do the most good, See-bastian," replied that enigmatic individual.

Billy had to be content for the moment with this answer.

"That's the Harlem River," exclaimed Billy suddenly.

"Now, ain't that nice!" came Mr. Smats' sarcastic voice. "I'm glad they still teach joggraphy in your school."

"But we started in the Bronx—what are we doing, riding around in a circle?"

"Boy, you'll have to save your questions for your teachers up at the academy in New Haven. This is the real thing, See-bastian. We're just takin' a few precautions to see if we're bein' followed. I'm old-fashioned and I've never been able to get used to machine-guns."

I stirred uneasily in my corner at this. It only then occurred to me that we might be in deadly peril, so preoccupied had my thoughts been with Julia. I wondered if I should ask Mr. Smats to drop Billy off? I knew Julia would never forgive me if I let the boy come to any harm.

"Is Billy really necessary to us—if there is danger?" I asked.

"See here—" Billy cut in indignantly.

I silenced him with a gesture.

"I should class See-bastian, now you put it to me," said Mr. Smats, "more as a luxury than a necessity—but that's only my private opinion. There're two reasons why we include him in the party—one, if we drop him off, they'd get him, too—and last, I guess the young lady will be kinda glad we brought him with us when we find her."

"Then we are going to find her?" I cried.

"If you think I'm ridin' in the night air for my health, you don't know my rheumatiz. Get this thing straight, Cornua. I'm going to find that girl—but don't expect me to find her at the next drugstore drinkin' a chocolate milkshake through a straw. You'll just have to leave it to me."

"You still think Killark and the police couldn't help us?"

"I think worse than that. If we called in the cops, we'd have to turn over our prisoners—Ed Flippenhauser and the headwaiter—to 'em. Then they'd be tempted to make things unpleasant for the little girl. But as long as we're in a position to meet 'em in a horse-trade, we'll be able to do business. I've sent 'em word there'll be no bulls in the party, and that gang knows me—my word is good. 'Course, that won't prevent 'em turnin' the iron hose on us if we give 'em a chance—hence the ride."

"Iron hose?" I inquired.

"Machine guns," replied Mr. Smats, and I felt a peculiar sensation travel again up and down my spine.

That a man of my retired life and philosophical tastes should suddenly, in the civilization of the twentieth century, find himself in danger of being fired upon by machine guns seemed too fantastically absurd. Yet Mr. Smats' manner was convincing, for I noted that he kept a sharp and incessant watch out the windows, an anxiety which belied the flippancy of his speech.

"Then we are going—where?" I asked. "I think I have a right to know that much, if we are to trust you implicitly in such a serious situation."

"Where it's safe—get me? And by back-country roads, so you'll have to excuse some joltin' later. I've got a little cabin, Cornua, up in the Connecticut woods that no one but me knows about. It's a dugout I've kept ready for an emergency. You know, in my business you have to think of everything—before it happens."

"Then we are not going to where Julia is?" I enquired, horrified at this new idea.

I had assumed that we were in pursuit of the thugs who had carried her off.

"It's hard to make newcomers understand a racket," explained Mr. Smats. "The Roslyn boys are following that trail, while the brains of the organization ducks for cover. Edith and Marybelle will keep the home fires burnin' at the office switchboard and I'll direct the job from a new headquarters."

"What will happen when the district attorney and the newspapers discover that Miss Gorland and I are missing?"

"If you ask me, I'll say it will start a very pretty guessing competition—specially as I'll be missing too—which you didn't mention—and See-bastian here, he'll be missing—so we'll be missing on all four cylinders. Strictly speaking, it's six, because the head-waiter and Ed Flippenhauser will be missing also—and if all these misses don't fill tomorrow's front page, I'll drink a cup of sassafras tea for breakfast."

"But won't it confirm the suspicion of my guilt?"

"It certainly will—you can bet on that, Cornua, if you can find any takers. But I figure it is better to be suspicious and keep your health than it is to have Ed's gang make a sieve of us. Then when we've settled this business and we turn up with Miss Julia and all the evidence, we'll ride up Broadway with the air full of ticker tape and go to Charley's for a steak and sea-food dinner."

"You are optimistically hopeful of a successful ending?"

"Cornua, I'm only human—and this is some crowd we are up against—but I've never been beaten yet—and we've got Ed in our hands, don't forget that ace in the hole."

"They have Julia," I cried.

"Correct. But Ed Flippenhauser is a whole lot fonder of himself even than he is of money—and that's saying a good deal. Don't you worry about the little lady—it's Ed who's going to do the worrying before I'm through."

There was something horrible in the thought of Julia as a pawn in a gang-war, but I kept my own counsel for the moment. What else could I do? Were not Billy and I also virtually prisoners, now that we had committed ourselves to going off with Joe Smats? Billy must have been thinking something of the same idea, for he cut in: "If you don't get results pretty damn soon after we get wherever we are going, Smats, I'll take a hand in this game myself."

"All right, See-bastian," calmly replied Mr. Smats. "Any time you feel like committing suicide, I won't put a straw in your path."

"Billy," I said severely, "for the present I hope that you will not interfere."

"All right, Uncle Robert," the boy replied, "but gee whiz, I can't help thinking about Julia."

"We are all thinking about her," I reassured him.

"In a day or two you'll find out I've done more than think," added Mr. Smats.

With this the boy had to be content, for as in my case, there was nothing he could do.

It was three forty-one a.m., when the car finally stopped. For the last hour and thirty-two minutes we had been driving along a series of winding and narrow dirt roads and it had not been possible to form much of an idea where we were. When we stepped out of the car I recognized the salt smell of the sea in the air and knew, for all the denseness of the woods in which we found ourselves, that we were not far from the shores of Long Island Sound.

Mr. Smats led us up a trail which he lighted for us with a small pocket flashlight. A figure suddenly stepped from behind a tree with a leveled automatic in his hands.

"O.K., George," said Mr. Smats.

The figure addressed as George lowered his pistol.

"I got the woods pretty well patrolled against surprises," explained Mr. Smats as we moved on. "And I don't mind passin' out as a piece of general information to whom it may concern, that it's just as hard gettin' out as gettin' in. You gotta have the right passport."

I understood from this slightly veiled remark that Billy and I were to consider ourselves as prisoners.

"But it's all for your own good," Mr. Smats added, as if to remove any suspicion of his purposes.

We passed two more sentries before, at the end of about a mile of wood trail, we reached a little cabin under a thick growth of trees.

"Can't even be spotted from an airyplane. I've tested that out," said Mr. Smats pointing with pride.

He knocked on the door.

"It's me, mother," I heard him say, "with a coupla guests."

The door opened and the amiable looking face of a middle-aged woman appeared in the illumination of Mr. Smats' flash.

"Well, it's about time," replied the amiable face, with a slight tartness of tone. "I never did like these spooky woods at night."

We were admitted to a pleasant rustic sitting room, lighted with oil lamps, but all windows I noticed were heavily curtained so that not a chink of light escaped.

"Mother, I want you should meet Mr. Cornua. This is Mrs. Smats," Joe said.

The lady graciously extended her hand. She was a large and ample person, with a kindly face. Her weight could not have been less than two hundred pounds.

"My! I've read a lot about you in the newspapers," she said heartily.

"And this is See-bastian, mother. Don't mind his name—he's one of these regular college football players."

"You don't say," exclaimed "mother."

"And now, mother, how about a bite to eat? We've all had a kinda tryin' evening, first and last."

"I guess I can make you up some turkey sandwiches, if you ain't too particular, folks. I haven't put the kitchen to rights yet, Joe's message only coming about an hour ago. And it's a pity leaving the shop just when business is beginning to be good at this time of year. Will you have yours on rye or white, Mr. Cornua."

I indicated my preference for rye as did Billy, and "mother" left the room.

"Sit down, gents," said Mr. Smats hospitably, "Mother'll be a wee might put out, but you musn't mind her. She had to leave her antique shop on the Boston Post Road at pretty short notice and you know women hate to move sudden. Besides, she's bound to do some worryin' over this Flippenhauser gang—you know that women is—always thinkin' the worst is goin' to happen and kinda disappointed when it doesn't. Well, Cornua, you have to take 'em as you finds 'em, I've always said," and Mr. Smats stretched his legs in a hickory wood rocking chair.

"It's too bad to bring her up here at this time of night just to look after us," I said.

"Say, you don't think I disturbed mother just so she can make sandwiches, do you? Why her shop will be the first place the crowd looks in at tonight—they know if they could lay hands on mother, they'd get me."

"Oh, I see," I said, liking less and less the ramifications of the maze in which we were involved.

"Mother" appeared in six minutes with a huge tray of turkey sandwiches, a pot of steaming coffee, and various plates of appetizing sundries such as sweet pickles and a variety of cheese. In spite of the peril hanging over us and the absent Julia, we all fell to with hearty eagerness, especially Billy, whose capacity to consume amazed even "mother."

"Land sakes, See-bastian," (she had adopted without question Mr. Smats' use and pronunciation of Billy's Christian name) "the next time I make you any fixings I'll get you some ostrich sandwiches—a turkey to you ain't a mite more'n a snipe to some folks."

"I'm sorry," said Billy flushing, a sandwich poised in mid-air.

"You just go right on and eat as much as you're a mind to, See-bastian. There's plenty more in the kitchen. Growin' boys needs plenty of victuals, especially when they ain't gettin' their proper night's rest. Mr. Cornua, won't you have a little of this cottage cheese—it makes a nice spread on that raisin bread."

"Thank you, Mrs. Smats," I said.

"You might as well call me mother up here in the woods, like all the rest. Down at the antique shop I get myself up to look like one of these pictures out of an old photygraft—cameo brooch and all—kinda gives a convincing background to my antique business— and I swear I get so used to playin' Mother Pine from Westforks for the benefit of the business, I forget we have a duplex apartment and a short wave set in the Bronx."

"Well, mother," said Joe Smats, "considerin' where you did come from—and how—you ain't steppin' much out o' your character when you play Mother Pine."

"I guess you're right, Joe. We have riz and no mistake."

"I'm strong for mother's racket, Mr. Cornua. Why she started in with a couple of broken chairs out of her attic and an old wooden bed my grandad died in, and in three years she's built up one of the biggest antique businesses on the whole Boston Post Road. Sales were three and a half truck loads last month, weren't they mother?"

"And mighty near one full load of hooked rugs besides."

Mr. Smats shook his head appreciatively and chuckled.

"When you consider, Mr. Cornua, that mother and me came off a couple of hard-scrabble Connecticut farms back in the Litchfield hills, where your best crops hardly kept the stock from starvin' to death—and just by puttin' our heads together we've built up two fine businesses—well, I don't want to blow my own horn, but I'm kinda proud of mother."

"Caskets and antiques," said mother. "Seems like the whole world has got to have 'em, one time and another. It was just commonsense, Mr. Cornua."

How much, I reflected, a philosopher can learn by unusual contacts with the world of human nature. In the future, I resolved to rely less on books in composing the concluding chapters of my manuscript.

"Now, Joe, before we all retire," Mrs. Smats interrupted my thoughts, "I want you should promise me you ain't goin' to get in wrong with the police in this business. After all these years we can't afford anything like that. They've never been able to hang anything on you, Joe, and I don't want they should start now."

"Mother, when I get through, they'll give me the keys of the city and a gardenia from Jimmy Walker for cleaning out one of the worst gangs they've got. Now don't you worry none—our children will always be able to look the world straight in the eye."

"Well, then, you mustn't pull somethin' too extra legal with Ed Flippenhauser. You're takin' an awful chance hidin' him and that other man away when the police is out lookin' for 'em."

"They don't know Ed Flippenhauser done it. When I turn him over with the evidence, it squares everything. 'Course, Killark will be a little put out, but I can fix that by giving him credit for the arrests."

"Well, you keep your eye peeled, Joe. You're treadin' in deep waters, don't forget that."

"You just trust me, mother."

"I guess it's about time you showed Mr. Cornua and See-bastian their quarters, Joe. I made up the beds in the room where your fishin' tackle is kept. It's the best we can do up here in this shack, Mr. Cornua."

"Thanks. We shall be very comfortable, I'm sure."

"We usually breakfasts around eight o'clock. Good night. If you'll excuse me, I'll straighten out the kitchen now."

With these words in our ears, Billy and I withdrew to the room assigned us.

# XV
## WAITING

I WAS AWAKENED by Billy's voice from the army cot opposite mine exclaiming "Came the dawn." I raised myself on one elbow, looked out the window at the woods beyond, and confirmed the statement. Already the sunlight was beginning to glint through the trees. I saw leaning against the trunk of a large maple one of Mr. Smats sentries, a dapper looking young man in what are known as snappy clothes, in short, hardly one's idea of a woodsman or of a gangster either for that matter. But it may have been significant that he kept one arm thrust inside his double-breasted lounge jacket.

"I suppose," I remarked, calling Billy's attention to the young man outside, "that that is a precaution against our using this window as an impromptu exit?"

"I imagine it works both ways," replied Billy. "It would be as hard for anyone else to enter by this window as it would be for us to leave by it."

"I have no desire," I replied, "to make a test of Mr. Smats' efficiency."

"I wonder what time breakfast is?" said Billy, preparing to enter the shower which occupied one corner of this rustic room

I gave a guilty start, for I had forgotten to enquire the precise time, beyond Mrs. Smats' vague 'round eight; and not to know the exact moment at which one is expected I have always felt to be an embarrassing predicament.

"Gee-ru-salem—this water is cold!" Billy chattered from beneath a downpour.

147

He emerged and began a vigorous job with a bath towel. I tried to make up my mind to equal his Spartan courage, while I admired the ripples of Billy's muscles over his athlete's body.

"There's a hot water tap, too," said Billy in answer to my thoughts.

I availed myself of this information and had what at my age is a more enjoyable bath.

We found Mr. Smats in the living room, his feet upon a table and in his hands a morning paper.

"The bull-dog edition just come through—they haven't any details yet, but plenty of headlines," and Mr. Smats offered me his paper.

"Cornua and Julia Slip Through Police Clutches," I read. "Murder Suspect and Girl Make Get Away. Police Have No Clues. Smats Missing Too."

"How about me?" said Billy, peering over my shoulder.

"You'll find yourself in the fine print at the bottom, Sebastian," said Mr. Smats.

"I say," cried Billy, "Dad will be awfully upset! I hadn't thought of that!"

"Yeah? Well, I guess dad will have to stand for it. He ought to of had more sense than send a son to college in the first place," replied Mr. Smats.

At this moment Mrs. Smats announced breakfast, which we ate in the kitchen.

"If there's one thing in this world that mother does well—it's waffles," said her husband, attacking a golden tower in front of him.

Amazingly enough we all ate heartily. I, for one, could hardly bring myself to realize the danger that involved Julia and all of us. Mr. Smats was his usual self; mother bustled about between oil-range and table; outside the sun was shining and the birds singing in the early spring of New England woods—before us were eggs, sausages, and unlimited waffles, not to mention coffee steaming from an old fashioned tin pot. Who could believe in peril, seeing it clad in such friendly and familiar garments? And yet, through the kitchen window I could still see the young man in snappy clothes leaning with apparent carelessness against the trunk of the maple.

"I'm leavin' you and See-bastian with mother for the day," said Mr. Smats, breakfast over and his ivory toothpick busily employed. "But when I come back tonight, there will be news."

"Now Joe Smats, you ain't goin' to stir a step," mother interrupted. "There's no sense in runnin' into danger and gettin' yourself arrested."

"Mother, there comes times when women folks has to keep their traps shut—and this is one of them," oracularized her husband. "If we just set here and did nothin', we would be sure up against it. Even Killark could find this place in about three days, so we've got to beat him to it. You don't suppose this is my idea of a vacation, do you, mother?"

"I'm not supposin' anything. You've all gone plum out o' your minds mixin' yourselves up in murders and things that don't concern you no more'n politics does my old tomcat. I never knew you to do such a thing, Joe Smats."

"Well, we've got mixed into this thing, mother, and we can't argue about it now. I'm off."

"Another time you'll listen to me before you answer phone calls from strangers in the middle o' the night," was her parting shot, some of the shrapnel of which spattered over me.

"I'll be slipping back when it's good and dark, because they may be followin' my trail by that time," Mr. Smats called from the door, "so don't worry if I'm a little late. If there's nothin' doin' by two a.m., you might have one of the boys slip down to a pay-station and call up Edith at the office—only tell him to watch himself gettin' back. Don't do any phonin' from around these parts—and I guess you better live on canned goods from the store shed. Don't do any marketin' today," and he closed the door.

"Now Mr. Cornua, you and See-bastian will have to excuse me," sighed "mother," "I've got my work to do. You just make yourselves to home in the livin' room—there's a parcel of magazines over by the window seat. We'll set down to dinner at noon."

I may have passed a longer day some time in my life, but if so, I don't recall it. Even "mother's" miraculous corned-beef and cabbage at twelve o'clock failed to cheer Billy up, although he consumed what was at least his fair share. Through the interminable afternoon I struggled with Billy's increasing restlessness. Had I not been firm with him, I believe he would have made a dash for it through the woods and probably have got himself shot.

Mrs. Smats was silent and uncommunicative all day. I believe her resentment against me, as the cause of her husband's predicament, grew steadily, but she was as attentive to our wants at supper, plying us with hot soda biscuits, honey, and green tea, as if we were convalescents requiring her special care. My own powers of making conversation were soon exhausted against the blank wall of her monosyllables, and by evening, Billy had sunk into deep gloom.

Always accustomed to consult my watch on all occasions, this day I found it in my hand every two or three minutes, but time, as usual, was inexorable and would not hasten for all my staring at a dial whereon it was registered. But often patience is more generous in its own reward than is virtue itself. The hands of my watch had crept around to one-fifty-two a.m., when the stillness, previously interrupted only by "mother's" snores from the depths of a rocking-chair was broken by a sound of voices speaking low outside the door. My ear had become acute from the strain of the day and I recognized one of the whispers as that of Mr. Smats. Before I could reach the door, it opened and in he came grinning broadly and with Julia on his arm!

Billy gave a yell that might have been heard a mile away and hurled himself at her, but she sidestepped him neatly and flung her arms about my astonished neck instead.

"Bobbie, Bobbie," she said, hugging me while she laughed and cried together.

I started to give her a cousinly kiss upon the brow, but she deftly substituted her warm lips instead—and for a moment my head swam. Then she turned and kissed the frantic Billy in an elaborately casual manner.

"Mother," I heard Mr. Smats say, "this is Miss Julia Gorland, last of the murder suspects."

"Pleased to meetcha, Julia," Mrs. Smats struggled up out of the rocker. "Would you like a cup of hot tea, dearie? You must be pretty well tuckered out."

"Thank you—that would be sweet of you."

Mother hustled off to the kitchen.

"But where—when—how?" Billy sputtered clinging first to one of Julia's hands and then the other.

"Now, you'll have to wait a little, Billy—until I've powdered my nose and had a cup of tea," said Julia pulling off her tight-fitting hat and shaking out the glories of her half-long copper hair. With this, she joined Mrs. Smats in the kitchen.

Mr. Smats stood grinning and slapping his thigh and making inarticulate noises to himself, apparently in sheer delight.

"Not a word," he said in reply to my look, "I wouldn't spoil that girl's story for an exclusive contract to bury all Harlem. Say, she's some girl—and don't you forget it. And it's one on the Flippen-hauser gang—this corner of the map will have a laugh that'll rattle the glasses in every speakeasy from Perth Amboy to White Plains when the yarn gets out. They'll not drive up to my front door and thumb their noses at Joe Smats again by kidnappin' any more of my friends—I'll bet 'em seven nickels to a rat-eaten doughnut on that. And she did it herself, dog my cats!"

Mr. Smats thereupon executed several steps of what I believe is called a "tap dance," at the end of which he gave Billy a resounding whack on the back.

"See-bastian," he said, "if you can cultivate as much brains and spunk as your girl has, you'll be Emperor of China some day."

"I know she's the most wonderful girl in the world," said Billy with naive simplicity.

"Right!" and Mr. Smats' hand smote Billy again on the shoulder.

At this moment Julia returned, accompanied by Mrs. Smats and the tea things.

"Just one cup, Billy," she said, "and then I'll begin."

# XVI
## JULIA'S STORY

JULIA SIPPED HER TEA with provoking slowness, but I saw by the merry dance in her eyes that she was thoroughly enjoying keeping us in suspense. Mr. Smats kept grinning appreciatively as one privileged to be in the know. "Mother" hovered about and plied her with hot buttered toast and other delicious things to eat.

"Now, if I was you, Julia," said Mrs. Smats, "I'd go straight off to bed and let these men folks hug their curiosity till morning, dearie. They've got you back and that ought to be enough for them for tonight. You might catch your death of cold if you get too tired."

"Oh, Mrs. Smats, I couldn't be so cruel! Look at their faces," giggled Julia.

"Was it awful?" Billy asked.

"Do I look as if it had been?" countered Julia, pursing up her lips. "Of course, it was a little scary at first, because I didn't know what they meant to do—but I kept my head because I realized a panic wouldn't help at all," and Julia meditatively bit a half-moon out of a slice of thin toast.

Her audience waited in breathless silence while she daintily crunched her toast.

"It's terribly embarrassing to eat toast in such a silence," she said. "I sound like a horse with a bag of oats. I'm sure the book of etiquette wouldn't approve—but I am hungry, Bobbie."

"Take your time, my dear," I said.

Billy was sitting on the floor at her feet, staring adoration up at her face. I saw her once lightly ruffle his brown hair with her hand—I looked away. I couldn't quite watch that. Mr. Smats did nothing but chuckle.

"Well," she began at last, "I was sitting outside in the limousine as you know—with your chauffeur Martin on guard, Bobbie—"

"Where is Martin?" I interrupted.

"I don't know," she said. "But he isn't important enough to come to harm, is he?"

"He'd be useful for identifications," mused Mr. Smats. "I guess he'll turn up all right."

"Oh, I hope so," cried Julia. "How stupidly selfish of me! I should have waited and brought him with me."

"Never mind now, dear," I reassured her. "We'll look out for Martin."

"Sure!" agreed Mr. Smats.

"I'll never forgive myself if Martin was hurt. But I'll begin at the beginning. It was really simple—the way they pulled my leg, I mean," Julia went on. "I saw the two girls leave— your wonderful secretaries, Mr. Smats—"

Mr. Smats coughed an interruption, with a slight glance at "mother."

"And in about five minutes two men came up to the car, opened their coats to show detective badges, and told me Mr. Killark was just back and wanted to see me at once on something very important at the house in the East Eighties. They said they would telephone you from the house, Bobbie, and send the car back for you. It sounded awfully plausible, because I knew you were expecting Mr. Killark—and these men had badges and everything—so I told Martin to drive us home. He protested at first—because he said he had positive orders from you, Bobbie, to wait. Of course, I was an utter fool, but I got very firm with Martin and told him I would take full responsibility. Besides, the detectives, as I thought them, were getting very impatient."

"I appreciate Martin's excuse now," I said.

"Well, I thought I had to be firm, Bobbie. So one man got in front with Martin and the other with me and we drove off. In a few minutes I noticed we were not going downtown—and then I saw through the glass that the man on the front seat had an automatic pressed against Martin's back—then I got frightened, Bobbie—just for a moment I was in a real panic—but before I could scream, the man beside me pushed a gun at me, and told me that 'one peep out of me' would cause him, to use the gun. He looked as if he meant it, so I began to think instead of risking a scream. Besides we were going pretty fast and no one would have heard me anyway. My first plan was to try to signal Martin to run the car into something and smash it up before we got out of the lighted streets. I was ready to take a chance on beating it during the mix-up—but I couldn't think, at first, of any way to get word to Martin. I had an idea I had to tap on the glass, as one always does, and that wasn't possible. That gun was pressed awfully tight into my ribs."

"Good God!" murmured Billy.

"Yes, dear, but he didn't shoot. That was another thing I tried to think out. Would he shoot if I tried something desperate? It was logical to suppose they wanted me alive—to trade for Mr. Smats' prisoners—so I decided at first that he wouldn't shoot, but then I thought they might kill Martin—so it wasn't any use taking that chance—besides they might shoot me in the leg or something—not where it was fatal—just to stop me if I tried to jump. It was terrible, Bobbie, because I couldn't make up my mind. I tried to remember something you'd told me about philosophy—always analyze a situation before acting, wasn't that it?"

"Yes, my dear child," I said.

"Oh, I'm so proud I remembered. The only trouble was that we were now out on the road somewhere going sixty miles an hour—and analyzing was using up a lot of country. And the only thing I could find to analyze was that there I was with a gun and rushing away from New York—which didn't help much. I didn't know before that analyzing could be so obvious—and turn out to have no answer at all."

"Analysis often reveals insoluble problems."

"Well, Bobbie, you never told me that—and I wasted a lot of time and brain work analyzing last night—that's all I can say. I think you ought to revise that part of your book and make it more practical. I kept saying to myself over and over again 'what to do—what to do' and getting hopelessly mixed up. Then I began to wonder if I could vamp these men—well, Billy, one has to think of things—"

This in reply to a gesture and slight movement from the boy at her feet.

"And I've read so many books in which girls did wonderful things with sex-appeal—it seemed worth trying, especially, Bobbie, as your analysis had failed completely—only I wasn't quite sure how to begin with a grouchy looking stranger who certainly had no sex appeal himself—to kind of lead me on over the first steps—and only a vicious looking pistol in his hand. And I saw he hadn't cleaned his fingernails and that put me off right at the start."

"The lousy bum," exclaimed Billy.

"Finally I got up my nerve and said to him he didn't have to hold that pistol so close against me, and I gave him a little look sideways like this—" and Julia illustrated with one of her delicious sidelong glances.

"Well?" urged Billy anxiously.

"It didn't work very well," Julia pouted. "He said: 'Hell, kid, don't try that stuff on me'—and jabbed me with his old pistol muzzle. I was just a little discouraged, but I gave him a smile as if nothing had happened. But he paid no attention except to try to light a cigarette with one hand while he hung on to the gun with the other. 'Let me hold the gun for you until you get a light,' I suggested to him, but he only gave me a dirty look, and the speed of the car kept blowing his lighter out. He said something under his breath that I won't repeat. Finally I felt almost sorry for him, so I said 'For goodness' sake, let me take the lighter if you won't trust me with the gun. I'll light the darned thing for you.' He seemed awfully surprised, but he let me do it. 'Now,' I said, 'all comfy?' when he puffed on the cigarette. That must have been a tactless remark because he said something very dreadful this time—not that I really cared. I'm broadminded about such things, you know, Bobbie, but I was getting a little peeved because he kept on being so cross. After all, one might as well have decent manners even if one is a kidnapper—there's nothing to be gained by grouching out of the corner of one's mouth."

"What then?" I asked, as Julia poured herself another cup of tea.

"I hadn't quite given him up, although it was pretty hopeless. I asked if I could have a cigarette, too, and reached for my hand-bag. He caught my wrist and flung me back with a bang against the back of the car. 'You touch that bag and I'll drill you full of holes,' he said. I was horribly angry because he had bruised my wrist—see, there's the mark."

Billy took her arm tenderly and gazed at a slight red spot on her forearm.

"I said, 'why you silly man, there's no call to get rough with me. There's nothing but my pocket book, a handkerchief, a vanity compact, a cigarette case and a lighter in that bag. I suppose you've got a complex on guns, but the girls in my crowd haven't taken to carrying them yet. I wish we did.' I tried to sound very sarcastic. He growled something and got me out a cigarette himself and stuck it between my lips with his dirty fingers. 'There you are, baby,' he said. 'Who are you calling baby?' I came back at him, for I was so mad by this time I had forgotten all about the sex-appeal I had been trying to work. 'You, sweetheart,' he replied and tried to get fresh."

Billy ground his teeth and said something which was quite the equal of anything in Julia's story she hinted she had suppressed.

"Well, I saw that I must stop that, so I tried bluff;" she contin-ued, with a reassuring smile at Billy. "I said to him: 'Ignatz, you don't suppose you can get away with kidnapping me'—I saw out of the corner of my eye that he did not like being called 'Ignatz'—'it's simply not done anymore—it's terribly old-fashioned—and that isn't everything. I'm as well-known by sight to all the police and reporters as Cleopatra's needle. I'll bet you you'll all be in jail in twenty-four hours.' Of course, I exaggerated a little, Bobbie, about how well known I was. He says, 'Say, sister,' (I think I preferred his calling me Baby, Billy) 'don't you suppose we know what we're doin'? We are not takin' you out just for a petting party. When your friends come across, we'll let you go, see? But you don't have to tell me we are taking one hell of a chance.' One good thing, he wasn't trying to be fresh any more. So I argued with him and suddenly I had an idea. The window behind Martin was open a little and I was certain Martin could hear me, if I spoke up. I cried 'I wish you wouldn't have my chauffeur run this car so fast, or we'll all be in the ditch.' I almost shouted the word ditch, but my captor seemed too dumb to notice, because he began telling me everything was O.K., and it wasn't much further. But I wondered if Martin had caught on. I pretended to cry and said again 'I know we'll be in the ditch.' I was watching the back of Martin's neck and his ears, for with the pistol jammed against him he was not likely to try to show me much of a signal. Well, Bobbie, I almost screamed for joy when Martin's head came back the tiniest little bit, not once but twice, slowly, showing it was not a coincidence. I knew Martin was a marvelous driver and would pick a place as safe as possible, but even so it would be taking a big chance. Still, Bobbie, the way I saw it, there was nothing left to take but a chance. I began to brace with my feet and watch the back of Martin's head. It would have to be at a place where he could slow down plausibly, for even Martin couldn't ditch a car at sixty miles an hour and hope for good results."

"Great heavens, my dear Julia, what a plan!"

"Didn't I tell you she was the real goods?" grinned Mr. Smats. "Nerve is her middle-name."

"The one thing I was really afraid of was being cut by broken glass, although I knew your car, Bobbie, had the non-splinter kind—and would they shoot Martin as he turned off the road before we had a chance to crash? Somehow I didn't think they would shoot me because I was only valuable to them alive, but they might not be particular about Martin. They didn't shoot him, Bobbie—it all happened too suddenly. We came to a sharp turn in the road which gave Martin his chance. He slowed down and I saw his head nod just once—then we went on over the turn, instead of around and landed almost upside down in a dense thicket of bushes. It was some smash and I almost had the wind knocked out of me, Billy—your poor Packard, Uncle Robert—but I wasn't cut and I wasn't hurt. I ducked just before we went over the top—you see, I knew it was coming and that's where I had the advantage over the man guarding me. I slid to the floor and then just as we left the road, scrambled out the broken window after we landed—it was a miracle I didn't cut myself then—and made full tilt for the heavy underbrush. It was black as ink, Billy, and I fell down no end of times, but I was away—and kept going. Soon I realized no one was after me—and I wondered about poor Martin—was he hurt? I almost went back—then I discovered I was lost in the dark and couldn't tell which way I had come."

"Do you think Martin was hurt?" I asked anxiously.

"I don't know, Bobbie—but like me, he knew it was coming. The man beside him went right through the windshield, I think."

"Land sakes alive," said Mrs. Smats.

"Some of the Roslyn boys is out looking for Martin," Mr. Smats interjected. "He wasn't reported at any hospital between New York and Boston today. I checked up on that."

"But how did you get out of the woods?" Billy enquired.

"By just walking, Billy—but I think I bumped into every tree on the way—you've heard of the man who couldn't see the wood for the trees—well, I couldn't see the trees because of the wood. It was dark as pitch—and then I stumbled on to where I saw some lights. I crept forward very cautiously because for all I knew where I was, I might be back at the wreck of the car—and suddenly I came out on a concrete road near a filling station. And Bobbie I jumped up and down and clapped my hands for joy—it was the road from White Plains to Mamaroneck—I knew it by the filling station where they had fixed a flat for me about two weeks ago. I walked in to the station and ordered three hot dogs and a cup of coffee. The men stared at me, and I must have been a sight with my clothes all torn and mussed from the crash and the tumbles in the wood. Just as I took a huge bite out of the first hot dog I had an awful sensation. There I was in the middle of the night without a cent—you see, Bobbie, I'd left my pocket book behind in the car—and with three hot dogs and a cup of coffee to pay for—to say nothing of getting a taxi to take me back to town. It was almost the last straw. However, I needed the nourishment, so I ate all three of the hot dogs and drank the cup of coffee before saying anything about paying for them—I even had an ice-cream cone, because it might as well be a sheep as a lamb. I didn't know what to do. Finally, I said 'I'm awfully sorry but I haven't any money.' That speech didn't make a hit at all with the man in the white jacket behind the hot dog griller. I was afraid it wouldn't. He shouted into the back room and an enormous man in shirt sleeves came out. He was sleepy and annoyed. 'I haven't any money,' I began again, 'and I owe forty cents. What will I do?' 'That's nize,' he says, 'you owe me forty cents and you ask me what you should do. You should pay and no monkey pizness. Vot you think I run, a free-lunch room already?' 'But don't you understand? I haven't any money.' 'Oi yoi yoi, you haven't any money, and you let the woman eat on credit, you dummer'—this to the man in the white jacket. 'Well, how the hell could I tell,' said he, 'she looked like a swell jane to me—only her clothes is mussed, but there's a lot of 'em walks home from auto rides around here and stops in for a dog on the way.' 'Is that a system?' wailed the proprietor, 'what you tink this is—a charity bazaar—you should give away free for nothing my hot dogs.' Well, Bobbie, I was getting frightened that this would be as serious as the other adventure. I remembered my little gold bracelet and bangle. 'This is at least worth forty cents,' I said with dignity, holding it out to the proprietor who was now shouting at the man in the white jacket.

"'Vot's this,' he said, 'somet'in you got at the five and ten?' and he took my bracelet—snatched it rather.

"'Say, don't you get rough with that lady,' said the man in the white jacket. 'Let me have your bracelet lady, and I'll pay this bozo the forty cents myself.'

"I was relieved at this sudden reversal on his part, but the proprietor had got him awfully sore during the argument.

"'Now where you want to go, lady? I'll see you home and this bird in hell, if he gives me any more of his lip,' said the man in the white jacket, who tore off his coat and hurled it to the floor.

"'Noo—you make a big talk—where's the forty cents?' the proprietor challenged.

"'Here,' said my defender, banging down some change on the counter, 'and for another two cents I'd smack you in the eye with one of these red hot Hamburgers.' I really thought he was going to do it for he picked up a sizzling wad of chopped meat and began making it into a sort of snowball.

"'Please let me out,' I said, making for the door.

"'I'll settle with you in the morning,' said my new escort, following me to the door and shaking his fist at the proprietor, 'when I call around for my paycheck—and see you have it ready, or I'll make this place look like the battle of Verdun."

"'You should worry about your paycheck, loafer. You owe me money,' and at these words I ran into the road, tired of the argument.

"But my troubles were not over, for my new escort came after me and joined himself firmly to my arm in the road.

"'Look here,' I said, 'I'm awfully grateful for lending me the forty cents and if you'll just direct me to a garage, I want to hire a car to take me home.'

"'I thought you said you had no money, kiddo,' he replied. 'And say, while I think of it, my name's Steve—Steve Rogsby—what's yours, baby?'

"You know, for the life of me, Billy, I couldn't think of a name—so I just had to say Julia.

"'Suits me,' said Steve, 'you can tell me the rest later, Julia,' and he actually had the nerve to squeeze my arm.

"'I must hire a car,' I said, trying to shake off his arm.

"Tony won't let a car out without the cash this time of night. What you're going to do, kiddo?'

"'That bracelet of mine you've got cost forty dollars. I'll come back and pay you tomorrow if you'll lend me some money and give me your address.'

"'I'd rather have your phone number, baby,' he said.

"I was getting really annoyed, so I turned on him and told him what I thought of him, and threatened to scream good and loud if he didn't let go of my arm. He took it all quite calmly and still held me by the arm.

"'Listen, baby,' he said, 'I've got a swell little canteloupe and I'll drive you home in that.'

"'A canteloupe?' I asked—how often you have scolded me Cousin Robert for my feminine curiosity.

"'Sure,' he answered, 'a rocky Ford—I call it a canteloupe because it's true—we couldn't. That's a hell of a joke, baby, but we gotta be friends.'

"'Well, you know, Billy, I began to think that perhaps this fellow wasn't so bad—vulgar, of course, but easy to handle, if I did it the right way—besides the road looked awfully dark and lonely—and I had no money—so I began cautious dickering.

"'Where is your car?' I asked.

"'In the garage back of my old man's—about a hundred yards down the road. Where do you live?'

"'New York.'

"'Sure, I know that, baby, but there's different addresses in New York—there's Coney Island and then there's the Ritz—you gotta trust me to drive you home, so you gotta trust me with your address. You've had to walk home from one ride tonight, baby, but you won't have to from two. I'll be good, so help me Santa Claus.'

"It occurred to me then, Bobbie, that if I told him to go to the house in the East Eighties the police would arrest us both—and turning up like that with a stranger would mix things up fearfully if we were arrested—to say nothing of getting this boy in bad when he had no connection with us. I didn't know what to do—it was just the same if I went to your apartment, Bobbie. It seemed as if every time I did anything, it couldn't be explained—it's all so horribly complicated. Then I had a bright idea. Why not drive to Mr. Smats' office—and take a chance. It wasn't likely the police would expect me there, although there was the risk it was being watched, too. So I gave the boy your address.

"'Just as you say, kiddo,' he replied, tipping his head to one side and looking at me out of narrowed eyes. 'I guess that's near a subway station, 'cause I know darn well, baby, you couldn't live in that part of the Bronx.'

"'Well,' I replied, 'it's where I want to go anyway.'

"'All right, baby,' he said, 'we'll leave it at that. Come on, we gotta get the old bus.'

"We walked down the dark road a short way to a little portable garage behind a small framehouse. Without a word he backed out an ancient explosive and wheezy coupe with bashed in mudguards, and I got in beside him."

"Well?" asked Billy anxiously as Julia paused and thoughtfully ate another slice of toast.

"He really did behave, Billy. Of course, he tried me out once—and I reminded him of his promise to be good.

"'I know you're a swell dame,' he said, 'and I'm only caretaker for a kennel full of hot dogs—what the hell—I know where I get off with a jane like you. Jees, it's a tough world—and God, I wish you was Clara Bow—or Alice White.'

"I felt rather sorry for the boy, Billy. He was starved for a little romance—and he wasn't so bad when you looked at his eyes. They were blue—a clean blue."

Billy groaned and writhed in his chair.

"After that, he told me his whole life history, Bobbie—how the girl he really wanted wouldn't look at him because she'd got a fellow with a bigger paycheck—and how he hoped to save up enough to own a filling-station and hot-dog stand of his own some day—perhaps, he said, he might build his place up to being a swell roadhouse in time—only now he had just lost his job and would have to begin again. I felt badly about this because he had lost his job on account of me, Bobbie, but I have his address and we can help him, can't we?"

"If he is as worthy as you think him, I'll gladly finance his venture," I answered.

"Well, he brought me back safe," said Julia. "I guess that's worth something."

"You bet it is," said Billy with sudden enthusiasm.

"I made him stop the car across the street from Mr. Smats' place of business—it was almost nine o'clock in the morning then—and I wanted to see if there were any police about. Then I gave him your address, Bobbie—and told him to write me there. He was as happy as if I had given him a million dollars—he really is a simple, sweet boy—I kissed him good-by, Billy—he deserved something—now

Billy, don't be silly—you know what I mean, it's no use pretending you don't."

"You kissed a guy who fries hot dogs?" asked Billy scornfully.

"Well, Billy—if you had asked me yesterday morning if such a thing was possible, I'd have thought it a joke. But I guess you never know what might happen," said Julia demurely.

"I'll just add a word," cut in Mr. Smats, as Billy pulled savagely at his pipe. "By one of them miracles talked about in the Good Book, the plain clothes detective didn't recognize Miss Julia. I figure it must have been the car she came in—they weren't looking for her to arrive in something off the junk pile. So Marybelle, who nearly had a fit when she realized who was calling, hustled Miss Julia here through one of my private doors in the cellar into the house next door—which is also mine, but even the cops don't know that. There's a back way into the house I use myself when the street gets congested with cops. Well, I was already there, having arrived before daylight, and I was able to fix up a quiet place for Miss Julia to rest in, on account we didn't want to leave until dark—and Marybelle and Edith gave her some fixings—"

"And I slept nearly all day," Julia put in, "that's why I'm not sleepy tonight."

"Most of the day Marybelle and Edith was being entertained by Mr. Killark—who kept searching my office and worrying the girls with questions—but those are two wise girls, Cornua, and all he found out was that I wasn't there. Then when it was good and dark Miss Julia and I came out the back way from the other house, step into another new car Mr. Killark has never seen—the license plates belong to a respectable delicatessen man—and drove back—and here we are. But they's one thing—we told Ed Flippenhauser his gang kidnapped Julia—and as they can't reach him to tell him different—we can still do business with him."

"What do you mean?" I asked.

"We'll pretend to trade him Julia's safety for his information—and he'll not know he is playing against marked cards," said Mr. Smats triumphantly.

## XVII
## WE COME OUT OF THE WOODS

THE NEXT MORNING I asked Mr. Smats to explain to us his plans. I was not looking forward to indefinite imprisonment in this cabin in the woods. Julia was sleeping late, worn out by her two nights of adventure.

"Fair enough," replied Mr. Smats to my request for information. "I'm going to make a deal with Ed Flippenhauser and then I'm going to lay the cards on the table for Killark. I figure on fixing Flippenhauser tonight, and tomorrow morning we'll drive to my place and let Killark arrest us all. It'll make him happy and not do us any harm, because by then we'll have the real dope. He'll probably want to stage a sensational arrest of Flippenhauser, so we'll fix that up for him, too. The customer must be satisfied—that's my motto."

"I don't relish the additional publicity for Miss Julia of having her arrested," I protested.

"Why, we won't be under arrest more than five minutes—and she'll have the time of her life. Young folks enjoy that kind of a party, Cornua. We could leave her behind here—but don't forget the Flippenhauser gang is working just as hard to locate us as Killark and his bunch of bulls. You wouldn't want Miss Julia to be in a gangster fight here. I wouldn't even leave mother behind."

"I suppose there is no other way?"

"Not a thing. The only slip up would be for Killark to get us before we straighten out Flippenhauser—and at that, I've told my Roslyn boys to let him come through if his men turn up in these woods. The guns are for the Flippenhauser crowd, Cornua. They won't be used against the police. There's nothing to worry about—because even if Killark did pinch us ahead of time, I can still turn Flippenhauser over to him and clear us all. But I want to go to Killark with a dead open and shut proposition—so you just keep your shirt on for another twenty-four hours."

I had no recourse other than to accept the situation as outlined by Mr. Smats. Billy and I spent a restless morning indoors, but were rewarded at luncheon by the appearance of Julia looking as dainty and fresh as though her experiences on the last few days had never been. "Mother"—Mrs. Smats, I mean—performed her usual miracles with the contents of the cans in the larder, and Mr. Smats, in his shirtsleeves, presided as host at the head of the table.

"I certainly will be glad of a mess of fresh spinach," said "mother," ladling out the vegetables. "I never did hold much with eating out of cans, save as a makeshift. Anything worth eatin' is worth taking pains with, my mother used to say. Seems like as canned goods in the Spring is a lazy way to set out a meal—but my land, when you can't do what you want, you've got to do the best you can. Have some more muffins, Mr. Cornua—they didn't come out of any package."

We had no newspapers because Mr. Smats felt that by now it would not be safe to send any emissary out of the woods, for in all probability every road would be closely watched by the opposition gangsters.

"Mother not being at the antique shop," he explained, "they'll figure we can't have skipped very far away because they'll know we want to talk to Ed Flippenhauser pretty soon. Besides, they don't know we've got Julia back, so they'll think we are somewhere in range looking for her—I guess they are too, figuring she couldn't get very far either. So you'll just have to hold your curiosity concerning your chauffeur and the guys in the ditched car. I'll bet that story makes a pretty spread today though."

"I hope Martin is safe," I said.

"Well, if you ask me, I think he's probably sitting in a cell in the Tombs with your friend Killark shakin' his fist in his face and ordering him to tell all. I figure it's kinda lucky Martin don't know nothin' to tell, 'cept that he disobeyed your orders with the usual results."

"Martin would allow himself to be drawn and quartered before he would betray any confidence of mine," I said, in defence of my servant.

"Maybe so, still I feel easier that he don't know our address up here in the woods. There's somethin' kinda persuasive about a blackjack."

Again, a long afternoon and evening dragged on. Mr. Smats dozed most of the time in an armchair, with a red bandana handkerchief over his face, from beneath which emerged the most amazing snores. Julia helped "mother" with the dishes and Billy joined when it was time to wipe them. After that, we all suggested a game of poker, with a ten cent limit, to Mr. Smats, arousing him for a moment from his slumbers.

"Thank you just the same, folks," he said, "but I'm a professional poker player. I'd do somethin' foolish in a ten cent game and that would hurt my pride."

At dinner Mr. Smats announced that about three a. m., we were all to start for his office in the Bronx in order to arrive at the back entrance through the next house before daylight.

"Lady Luck, be good to us—just this once more, and I'll let you off my prayers for the rest of my life," he added at the end of his plan of action.

I took him one side.

"You mean there is danger for Julia in this trip?"

"You bet—and for all of us. We may get a sprinklin' from a machine gun—and we may not. Depends on the Flippenhauser gang havin' found the trail—"

"In that case—" I began.

"In that case," he interrupted, "we wouldn't have any more chance if we stayed here than a snowbird in hell—so I prefer to make a dash for it. And after this is all over, I'm goin' to take a vacation in Paris where a guy can drink his shots instead of gettin' 'em served with lead."

Mr. Smats further proposed that for various reasons Julia should dress in man's attire. To my surprise, she welcomed this suggestion as great fun.

"I'd like mother to do the same," he added, "only there ain't a pair of pants on earth that would look plausible on mother."

"Why Joe Smats," was her retort to this statement, "I ain't as fat as some folks I know."

"No," said he, "but they mostly travels with circuses, mother. But we don't need to argue about that now. Trouble is, you're too good a cook."

"Mother" appeared pacified by this compliment.

Julia soon entered, dressed in a suit of rakish looking clothes that Mr. Smats had produced from a cupboard.

"I got them in case I wanted to disguise myself as a college boy," he explained. "I couldn't think of nothin' that would be a more complete disguise for me."

Julia turned and twisted looking at herself in the small mirror in the living room, evidently delighted with this new adventure.

"What do you say, Billy?" she asked, crowding her copper hair up under a felt hat.

Billy looked more things than he seemed capable of expressing.

"Ready folks?" said Mr. Smats from the door.

"Just a second," cried Julia, and she began vigorously scrubbing her lips and cheeks to remove the quite unnecessary touches of lipstick and rouge I have never been able to persuade her to give up.

We went cautiously single file down the winding trail, preceded and followed by a considerable number of Mr. Smats' guards—or "Roslyn boys," as he preferred to call them. Not a sound broke the stillness of the dark, moonless night, save an occasional twig snapping underfoot. Strict silence had been enjoined upon us all. We reached a large, closed limousine standing ready in the wood road, without having seen even the fleeting shadow of a foe. But I confess that my heart had been in my mouth the whole way through the woods, half expecting the flash of a shot from every bush we passed. Julia and Billy had walked very close together.

Quickly we packed ourselves into the car—the dimensions of "mother" making the word "pack" an appropriate one. With a low purr the car shot forward swiftly as the door closed.

"Well, here we are," said Mr. Smats, wiping his face. "The worst is over, folks. All hell on wheels couldn't catch us now, but if there's any shootin', Julia and Mother will lie flat and face down on the floor—and stay there. Get me?"

When we left the wood lane at last and turned into the Boston Post Road and its traffic stream, Mr. Smats waved his hat.

"Three cheers, folks!" he cried. "We've got out of the tightest hole any of us will be in again for some time."

"Joe, you said a mouthful," commented "mother." "After this, I'm goin' to see you lay off murder cases, meanin' no disrespect to present company—but we're gettin' too old to run risks. We've got our antique business and we've got our undertaking parlors—and those profits are enough for any decent, respectable folks."

"How'd you like to go to Paris for Christmas, mother?" queried Mr. Smats. "I hear tell they got a wonderful morgue over there."

"Now, Joe Smats—when we take a vacation, you're going for a real rest. I won't have you hangin' around no morgues and talking shop all the time. I don't mean to look at a single antique in any of them museums. We'll just run around to cabarets and look at live ones."

"Suits me—considering what kind of live ones they've got to look at in them Pareesian cabarets."

"Joe, you're always twistin' my words around. Of course you can look your fill at the French cuties of you've a mind to—but remember, I don't choose to stand for no funny business."

At this point, I coughed discreetly, for I felt the conversation was getting somewhat too intimately domestic for Julia's ears to hear.

It was exactly three minutes to five when the car stopped by the back entrance to Mr. Smats' quarters. We entered the house that was connected with his offices by the secret door in the cellar, and as the entrance was on another street and the secret safely kept, there was no gauntlet of watchers to run.

"The main entrance is probably unhealthy," said Mr. Smats, as we passed through several heavy doors equipped with spring locks, to find ourselves in a suite of pleasantly furnished rooms. "Got your bag, Julia?"

"Yes."

"Well, step in there and put on your regular clothes. We don't want Killark and the newspaper boys to see you like that."

Julia obeyed.

"Now, I'm going out—alone—to see Ed Flippenhauser and have the showdown with him. When I come back we'll all go into my office next door and let Killark walk in and arrest us. And he'll do it with bells on—boy! I can just see him doing it now."

"Is it safe for you to go out?" I asked him.

"No—but I gotta go. I figure it won't be safe until somewhere around ten o'clock, when we've settled the whole business. You just try to keep mother from worrying too much while I'm away, Cornua. And I'm sorry breakfast will be late, but we can't take any chances gettin' in food."

"I made up a parcel of sandwiches and brought 'em along," said "mother."

"Now just sit tight," was Smats parting injunction. "Keep away from windows—leave the shades down. Don't get excited. So long."

Mr. Smats vanished through the first of the massive doors, leaving "mother," Billy, Julia and me to stare at one another with a wild surmise.

# XVIII
## WE ARE ARRESTED ONCE MORE

IT WAS ELEVEN MINUTES to ten precisely when the massive doors re-opened to admit the return of Mr. Smats. All of us, according to our several temperaments, expressed our relief and our joy at his safe arrival.

"And folks," he said, "we are all set for the grand finale. Now put on your wraps, mother, and you too, Julia, and bring any little fixin's along you women folks is likely to need, and we'll go into my office and let Killark do his stuff. That'll be act one—flourish of police whistles—chorus of cops with nightsticks—Julia here as the heero-ine—Cornua, poor but honest friend, Billy the guy that sings the tenor solo in the moonlight, mother worryin' in the background, and Joe Smats, the honest mortician, smoothin' away all the difficulties of the plot, with song and dance specialty—show girls by Edith and Marybelle. How's that suit you?"

"What will be act two?" I asked, smiling in spite of myself at Mr. Smats' exuberance of spirits.

"Phee-nominal and sensational arrest of Ed Flippenhauser by the ass-tute detective, Killark of the Homicide Squad—with grand chorus of newspaper reporters, and scenery by the tabloid news photographers."

"Land sakes, Joe Smats, do talk sense," said "mother."

"Sense? I'm talking nothing else but. Last act, happy ending, to be wrote by Julia and See-bastian, who will appear in person and personally. Now, that's enough idea of the plot of this stupendous spectacle—let's get at it."

170

We all followed Mr. Smats through the secret passage and door leading into his known and advertised place of business, where the two blondes, Edith and Marybelle, ushered us into Mr. Smats' private office.

"Now you two girls show Killark right in, as soon as he comes—just tell one of the plain clothes boys out front there's somethin' doing so he'll phone Headquarters—because we don't want to keep the ladies waitin' till the spirit moves Killark to call. He's liable to rush off to San Francisco on a hunch and leave us all flat."

Mr. Smats then proceeded to pass his casket of cigars to Billy and me and we settled back in the luxurious chairs of his inner sanctum to wait with such patience as we could command. Billy and Julia sat very close together and appeared able to communicate quite satisfactorily with one another without uttering a sound. Mrs. Smats got out some knitting and proceeded placidly with something in grey wool. Mr. Smats ran through a pile of letters on his desk. I placed my fingertips together and tried to reflect upon the situation, for I was not entirely free from anxiety over the outcome, and was particularly dissatisfied with the inevitable publicity that was certain to ensue.

I ventured to make one last plea in avoidance of this unpleasantness, in case there was any way it could be obviated.

"A man in your position can't butt into a murder-case, Cornua, and not attract attention," said Mr. Smats, "any more'n you could carry off the Statue of Liberty and expect no one to miss it."

I was forced to confess that Mr. Smats undoubtedly spoke the truth.

We waited exactly thirty-seven minutes, at the expiration of which time, we heard an infernal din outside. Gongs clanged, sirens shrieked, whistles blew, and then Mr. Killark accompanied by what seemed a regiment of blue-coated policemen burst open the door and the air was literally filled with leveled revolvers.

"Put up your hands—everybody—it's part of the game—and some of these boys look a little nervous," warned Mr. Smats, as the police swarmed in.

We obeyed. In the rear I saw the two girls, Edith and Marybelle, handcuffed and held by two policemen each. This time Mr. Killark had determined to be thorough.

"Pile 'em all in the wagon, boys," sang out Mr. Killark.

"Just a minute—just a minute," said Mr. Smats. "Don't forget to turn on your powers of deduction, Killark. Why do you suppose we are all here—including mother—where even a bell-hop from a hotel could find us? There must be a reason."

"I haven't time to talk," snapped Killark, and one of his men clicked handcuffs on Billy and me. At least this permitted us to lower our arms. But the order to take us to the patrol wagon hung fire.

"That's too bad, because if you don't talk to me, you won't find out who killed Howard Birmingham and shot Grierson, the butler— which I take it, is the main object of your call."

"Do you mean you want to confess here and now?" asked the detective, rotating his cigar a three-quarters turn.

"Well, I *have* got a confession to show you, and I've got a guy stowed away who is going to turn state's witness—motive, cold feet—and the whole solution, only don't get rough, or I'll get mad."

"Make it snappy then."

"Can I put my hand in my pocket and get out a paper?"

"No."

"Then just reach in the top left hand side, will you? It's folded lengthwise—and I think you'll recognize the signature."

Mr. Killark strode up to Mr. Smats, while an officer jammed the muzzle of a revolver against the mortician's ribs.

"Let me know when I can lower my hands," said Mr. Smats as Killark took the paper. "I got a touch of rheumatiz in my left elbow."

"Frisk him," said Killark to an officer, while he frowned over the document.

"Of course, I haven't got a gun," smiled Mr. Smats. "I didn't want you to get funny with me over the Sullivan law—as for Seebastian there, he's too occupied to think of carrying a gun—and Mr. Cornua, he's just plain afraid of fire-arms. That's the kind of a desperate gang we are, Killark. You don't suppose there's a pineapple hidden in mother's knitting, do you?"

"Ed Flippenhauser—the international crook, eh?" said Killark in an altered tone of voice, when he reached the signature. "Pretty clever forgery, Smats, but my leg don't pull that easy."

"It's painful for you to admit it, Killark—I concede that, but I've solved this little mystery for you—and I can prove it. I can take you where Ed Flippenhauser is—and I've got the headwaiter from the Garden of Aphrodite as state's evidence."

"Yeah? Well, you can't bluff this time, Joe. Ed Flippenhauser isn't going to wait for me to come, even if this isn't a forgery."

"Oh yes, he is," replied Smats. "I'm Joe Smats, knows all, sees all. I've kept Ed in a kinda informal arrest ever since some of my honest Roslyn boys picked him up for me. Now, if I take you there, you won't hold any informalities or irregularities concerning his detention against me or the Roslyn boys, will you?"

"I can arrest you for not turning your information over to the police at once."

"Now, be reasonable, Killark. I didn't get that confession from Ed until this morning—and soon as I had it, we all came straight here. I can prove that by these witnesses."

"Why did you spirit these people away, when they were legally under police surveillance?"

"I'm about as much of a spirit as Houdini ever found. I suppose you'd like to have had 'em shot by the Flippenhauser gang? Well, I figured they'd be more useful to you alive—specially as you was off in Chicago ridin' around in a sight-seeing bus. The only spiritin' that was done, was pulled off by Ed's crowd when they had the nerve to drive right up to my front door and kidnap Julia. I've never been so insulted in my life."

"A plausible yarn! How'd you get Miss Gorland back?"

"She got herself back, havin' more gumption than some folks I know. I guess Martin told you the first part of the story."

"He does stick to a rigmarole about kidnapping and smashing up a car—story isn't possible."

I gave a great sigh of relief at this revelation that Martin was safe and sound, though in the hands of the police.

"Isn't possible, eh? Well, you try to kidnap a modern girl, Killark, and you'll find out some things you never figured on. She'll testify when the time comes, don't you worry about her."

"Certainly, Mr. Killark, I'll be glad to tell all I know," said Julia.

"It's about time some of you police got a little common sense," remarked "mother." "The idea of making all this fuss when all you got to do is arrest Ed Flippenhauser and find out the truth."

"A four cylinder doesn't pick up as fast as a straight eight," mused Mr. Smats aloud.

"Joe, I'll look into this—but I warn you—if there is any flim-flam about it, you'll not get off this time. I'm getting pretty damned sick of your tricks."

"When you play pinochle, cap, there's more to it than just holdin' the cards. Now I'll tell you one thing—I got Flippenhauser's confession on a kinda bluff—you see, he thought his crowd still had Julia—here's the order for her release—it will put you in touch with some of the missing gunmen, Killark. What made it possible to corner him is the headwaiter's story—here it is. The game being up all round, I persuaded Ed that to hold Julia would make matters worse for him. So he's all ready to plead insanity and call it a day."

"You mean he will repudiate this confession?"

"Sure thing. It ain't official—or sworn to, although I am a no-tary public—that was askin' too much. But I wanted the other paper about Julia so you could pick up the rest of the crowd."

"Would it be in order," I asked, "to read the Flippenhauser confession aloud? Some of us present are rather eager to know the circumstances relating to Mr. Howard Birmingham's death."

"It hasn't been verified, yet, Cornua. I'm not sure this isn't a put up job," replied Killark. "The whole thing may be an invention."

Mr. Killark shifted his cigar from the east side to the west and stared aggressively at each of us in turn. Mr. Smats hummed a tune and lightly clinked his handcuffs in time to the air. Then the great detective read the confessions in his hands slowly once more. I waited in some anxiety for the oracle to give utterance.

"Bring those two blondes in here," Mr. Killark suddenly commanded.

Edith and Marybelle were brought in.

"Everybody been frisked?" he asked.

"O.K., not a thing, chief," acknowledged one of the police.

"Then take the handcuffs off the whole crowd and hold 'em in this room until I return with Joe Smats. Tell the newspaper boys outside somethin' big is breakin', but don't let 'em in here. Don't allow these people here to talk to each other until I get back."

There was a general clinking in the room as handcuffs were removed.

"Gee, look at that!" cried Marybelle, "you made a great red mark on my wrist, you clumsy boob."

"Shut your face and keep it clamped down," replied Mr. Killark. "Now then, boys, send squad B along with me and Smats," and Mr. Killark left the room followed by Joe Smats between two policemen.

"Please, can't I say just a word?" asked Julia of a policeman who sat in a chair and stared hard at a colored print of Venus rising from the Sea over Mr. Smats' desk.

"You heard my orders. You'll have to be patient, lady," he said.

"Not a little, tiny word?"

"Orders, lady, orders."

Julia sighed and she and Billy resumed their silent communication. Marybelle and Edith got out their vanity kits and repaired the damage done by rough handling and handcuffing. "Mother" took up here knitting again, and I, as usual, had nothing to do.

## XIX
## MR. SMATS SUMS UP

DURING THE ABSENCE of the detective and Joe Smats I had been more worried about Julia than over the outcome of our present predicament. The photograph of her mother that had been found in Howard Birmingham's watchcase had never been explained. If all the truth were now to come out, as seemed probable, would the ideal memory of her mother be shattered? Suppose that Grierson had murdered Birmingham for some sordid revenge? I feared the effect of such a shock upon her. And yet there was no way. I could protect her, or shield her from whatever knowledge might come out.

At sixteen minutes after one, Mr. Killark and Joe Smats returned, the latter with his face illumined by one of his cynical smiles, Mr. Killark very brisk and business-like.

"First, I want to apologize to Miss Gorland and you," he said. "No hard feelings, I hope, but thanks to your interference, Mr. Cornua, the circumstantial evidence was very strong. We'll just drive down to the District Attorney's office and straighten out the technical details."

Billy let out a yell of delight and hugged Julia. Everyone, including Edith and Marybelle, crowded around us and shook Julia's hand and then mine.

"I'll say just this, Cornua," said Joe Smats, "you're so covered with horse-shoes nothin' can hurt you. Four days ago I'd a bet seven to one you'd travel up the river."

At the district attorney's office, whither we all journeyed, the mysteries were finally revealed—and like all mysteries, turned out to be simple when one knew the facts. I shall set them down in Mr. Smats' own words, since it was he who really had been our deliverer. Mr. Smats' summing up, which I am about to quote, was delivered that evening at my apartment in Park Avenue, where the astounded Evans served dinner at precisely seven-thirty to Mr. and Mrs. Smats, Billy, Julia and me. Outside, holding the door against reporters, was the faithful Martin, my chauffeur, restored once more to his proper rank and privileges.

"The night I come into that house and see what had happened," Mr. Smats began, "I saw right away that you and Julia couldn't have done it—we old hands can always tell this much—who didn't do it. But, of course, it was mighty funny your wantin' to hush it all up. I couldn't figure that out, because it wasn't reasonable—'course, now I know you, Mr. Cornua, it's different—I understand now—it was just your way of trying to be helpful. But it upset all my theories. And I thought, maybe, there's something funny in the will and you was figurin' on doing Miss Julia out of some of the money. Well, I had a kinda disinterested attitude, except I doped out that I could make you pay pretty well for whatever you was trying to pull off.

"Then when I got a look around the house after you and Julia here had left to go to the Garden of Aphrodite, I gathered up some clues which I said nothin' about, puttin' 'em away to protect myself if I got wedged in the jam."

"Why, Joe Smats—you never said a word to me about 'em," Mrs. Smats interrupted in a grieved tone.

"No more I did, nor to anyone else, mother. I didn't know which way the cat was goin' to jump then, remember. But I found out Grierson killed Mr. Birmingham, and I differed from Killark in his hunch because I had the proof."

"For heaven's sake, man," I cried, "why didn't you produce it?"

"Well, in the first place, you was payin' me, Mr. Cornua, to keep my mouth shut—and I wasn't sure yet about your share in the thing—perhaps I was being paid because you had something with Grierson—how could I tell? And second, there's not much love lost between me and Killark and I thought I'd let him rastle his own clues for a while. Then I'm a son of a gun, if they didn't go and shoot Grierson. That mixed all my calculations up, and I decided to lay low, particularly as I knew Killark would ramp around considerable. By hanging on to my proof, I could let myself out the back door any time things got too hot. You see, Mr. Cornua, I'm a man of my word and I meant to go through with what you was payin' me to do."

"Right, Joe Smats," cut in "mother." "You couldn't look your Lord in the eye if you wasn't. They don't call him the square mortician for nothing, Mr. Cornua."

"Then I was kinda wondering about Miss Julia here. It was not until I see See-bastian that I concluded nobody was working an inside racket on her—you, for instance, Mr. Cornua. See-bastian wanted to get elected to the Roslyn Club—gosh, that was a good one!" and Mr. Smats smacked his thigh vigorously.

I checked Billy's comment.

"Well, I was treed by the killing of Grierson, and the waters looked kinda deep. I wasn't too ready to dive in, until you come up to my office with See-bastian and I realized Killark was out to get me. You see, if he didn't solve the murder mystery, he'd have to make some other kind of a play—and gettin' me and the Roslyn boys would be a pretty good counter attraction.

"So, thanks to See-bastian seeing that headwaiter on the subway platform, I was able to take some active steps on my own. Up to then, the blackmail of Miss Julia might have been done by any one of four or five gangs, and everybody had crawled into a hole while the newspaper ballyhoo was on. I didn't know—the boys didn't. But when we located this guy, we knew—we found out from him it was the Flippenhauser bunch.

"If Ed had played fair and cut up that hundred and fifty thousand right, we'd never untangled things—but Ed had to get the headwaiter sore by only giving him a measly grand. So he was ready to make trouble for Ed.

"Now I was all set for my big play, when what does this gang do but come right up to my own front door and kidnap Miss Julia. Good night! Nobody ever pulled anything like that on me and got away with it. An insult—that's what that was—an insult to my intelligence! If Ed had stopped to think, it wouldn't have happened. He'd have known better—but he figured it would help him. Well, before I could tend to that myself—and by the way, the guys that carried you off, Julia, was shaken up and cut some, but not what you'd call really hurt—one on 'em lost some teeth, he claims—well, Julia takes care of herself. Now there would be shootin' and gunplay if us and the Roslyns got caught in a cross fire with the Flippenhauser gang and Killark's bulls, specially after the kidnapping, so I took everybody off to the cabin in the woods where we'd be safe for a spell—till I could settle things. I'd still got to find out about shootin' Grierson or I didn't have a complete story for Killark.

"The danger, as I told you, Cornua, was from the gang—not from the police. So I goes in and dickers with Flippenhauser, he thinkin' his crowd has Julia still. 'Course, there was a chance some of his crowd might spot me and bump me off, and then we would be complicated. Killark would have probably first-degreed you, Cornua. But it didn't happen because I'm a cautious cuss when I have to be, which is most of the time.

"Now Flippenhauser stuck to it that shootin' Grierson was a mistake—like we all thought it was, remember? And he did me the compliment to say that the guy they meant to get was me."

"Why you?" I asked.

"Bless your innocent ignorance, Mr. Cornua, because the boys had reported my entrance into the house and scared 'em pink. Eloise—you remember her?"

"My maid," exclaimed Julia.

"Sure—well, she was planted by Ed inside the house to give him dope—and she had signalled before you went to the Garden of Aphrodite that Mr. Birmingham had been killed.

"At first, Ed very nearly called his blackmail party off, for fear of getting a murder hung up with it. Then he ordered it carried out because one hundred and fifty thousand was a lot of money to throw away. And you, being in the house, gave him another idea. But when I came into the picture, they was scared for fair. They figured you,

Mr. Cornua, as wise enough to know where to get help. They might get away from the bulls, but me and the Roslyns was something else again. So they calculated that after I'd fixed up the body, I'd be certain to go back to the office—and there was my car and everything waitin' outside, showing I meant to come out. Ed sent orders to get me when I did, thinkin' he'd stop trouble at the source. They wasn't thinkin' of Grierson, not knowing him from the man in the moon.

"Well, Grierson steps out and gets the garden hose sprayed on him—some boob was nervous and fired before he checked up he had the right party. Havin' made that mistake, they couldn't stick around any longer, so all hands beat it for cover—where they stays."

"That explains Grierson's death," I said, "but why did he kill Mr. Birmingham?"

Mr. Smats lit one of my cigars, sipped a little from his fourth demi-tasse—Evans' hand had trembled the last time my eyes had ordered him to fill Mr. Smats' cup once more—and gazed at the ceiling.

"I've turned the letters and papers I found in Mr. Birmingham's wall-safe over to Killark," said Mr. Smats, still gazing reflectively, at the ceiling.

"You opened his wall safe?" I asked in astonishment.

"Well, it was a pretty easy one, and it was a trick I learned when I was a young man. Handy, but I don't use it any more. And I didn't tell Killark I got 'em there—desk drawer, I said. Grierson had been blackmailing Howard Birmingham for a good many years—he'd forced himself on him as butler among other things—and I found records of payments—as much as ten thousand at a time. Something about some mining interests and claims long ago—among something else—remember those old gold jewelry we found on Grierson?"

"Yes—and the picture—the photograph, you mean that we found on Howard Birmingham?" I said impulsively, then could have cut my tongue out as I saw Julia sitting there, her large eyes staring at me.

"The one in the watch-case? I guess so," said Smats.

"What on earth are you talking about?" asked Julia. "I gave Uncle Howard mama's picture for his watch myself—when auntie died and he was feeling lonely. I was only a child—and when he said he had no picture of auntie, I brought him one of my mother instead—to make up for it—it was a child's idea—but he was pleased—cut it out and put it in his watch—and always wore it because I'd given it to him."

How humbled and mean I felt over the suspicion that had been in my mind! I was ashamed to think that I had accepted flimsy circumstantial evidence like any untrained mind.

"Well," said Mr. Smats, "Grierson had a hold—that's all we need to know now, I guess—and the day came when Mr. Birmingham refused to go on with the payments. Grierson came back from his afternoon off, through the back door, while Julia was downstairs, and Birmingham caught him in Julia's room, rummaging among her things—perhaps for more evidence for blackmail purposes— he probably found out about Flippenhauser's stock market racket from your maid, Miss Julia. That's where Birmingham caught him, in your room, and in a frenzy of rage during the row that followed, Grierson snatched up the manicure knife off the dressing table and killed Howard Birmingham."

"Strange," I murmured.

"Not very," said Mr. Smats. "He hadn't planned it, you see—at least, not then. Rage—hate, that's all. Killark saw at once it was an inside non-professional job, and that the blackmail was an outside, professional one—but he couldn't prove it because I had all the proof. I beat him to it. But he had to hang on to you, Cornua, to save his face. That's how I've come to win your fifty thousand dollar reward."

"You've earned every cent of it," I said. "I don't grudge it a bit."

"Well, mother, how about going down tomorrow and making a steamer reservation for Paris? 'Course, we'll have to stay for the trial of Flippenhauser and his gang, but that won't take long— there's no first degree charges against Ed, seeing as the shooting was not planned. Ed's going to take his stretch, figurin' that'll interrupt business less than fightin' the case."

"I think we better be goin', Joe. Time's runnin' on late and we ain't had a proper night's rest for some time."

So with grateful handshakes and a joke or two, Mr. and Mrs. Smats left.

Billy rose and took Julia by the hand.

"I guess I'll see Julia back to the house in the East Eighties."

"Do, my boy," I said, and my eyes dimmed a little as I looked at these two happy children.

"Can we have a very quiet little wedding—Uncle Robert?" Julia asked. "Do you think it would be wrong, so soon after Uncle Howard's death?"

"Of course not, dear," I answered, swallowing a lump.

She flung her arms about my neck and kissed me.

"Good-night, Bobbie."

"Good-night, Julia dear. Good-night, Billy."

The door closed after them. Evans stood at attention.

"Anything else, tonight, sir?"

"No, Evans. Tell Martin to take the car back to the garage after he has driven the young people home."

"Yessir, thank you, sir."

I sat down before my desk, the pages of my manuscript on *The Philosophy of Human Nature* lying before my eyes. I looked up at the clock. It was exactly seventeen minutes and thirty-three seconds after midnight.

# Coachwhip Publications

## CoachwhipBooks.com

CLUES AND CORPSES

The Detective Fiction and
Mystery Criticism of Todd Downing

CURTIS EVANS

ISBN 978-1-61646-145-4

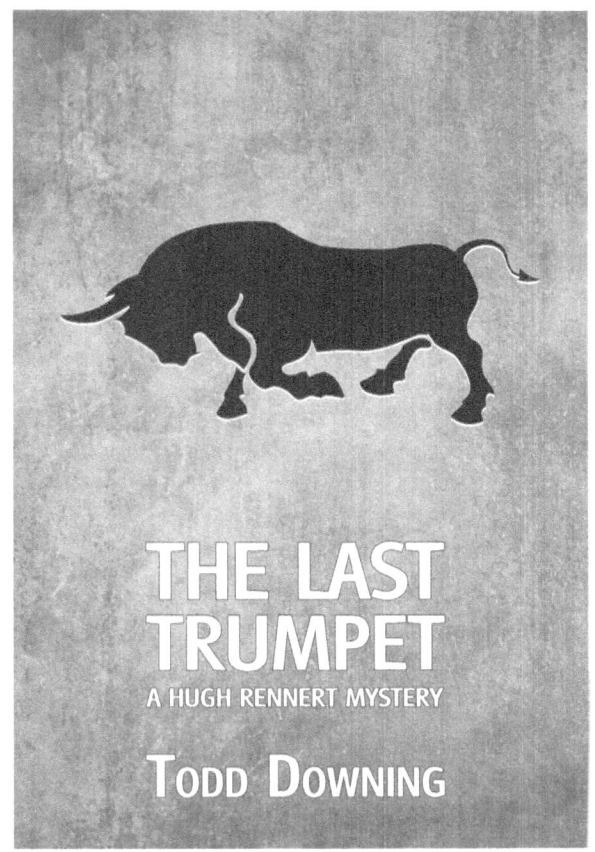

THE LAST
TRUMPET
A HUGH RENNERT MYSTERY

TODD DOWNING

ISBN 978-1-61646-152-2

# Coachwhip Publications

## CoachwhipBooks.com

ISBN 978-1-61646-222-2

# COACHWHIP PUBLICATIONS

## ALSO AVAILABLE

THE QUINNY HITE
MYSTERIES
CHINESE RED · HERE LIES THE BODY

RICHARD BURKE

ISBN 978-1-61646-247-5

COACHWHIP PUBLICATIONS

COACHWHIPBOOKS.COM

MURDER OF
THE HONEST BROKER

WILLOUGHBY SHARP

ISBN 978-1-61646-211-6

COACHWHIP PUBLICATIONS

COACHWHIPBOOKS.COM

ISBN 978-1-61646-232-1